A P

Book 2 of

A Victorian Romance

Lana Williams

USA Today Bestselling Author

Prologue

ondon, England 1870

L   Lady Tabitha Malton's stomach fluttered with nerves as she entered the emergency meeting of the Mayfair Literary League. In the year since she'd been a member, they'd never held anything other than the normal monthly gatherings. She couldn't imagine what had happened that called for an urgent summons.

The other five members of the book group were now dear friends. Considering how few friends Tabitha had, that made them particularly special. She would do anything for them and knew they felt the same.

Lady Phoebe Fitzroy, their host, was one of her closest friends. From her grave expression, something of weighty consequence had occurred.

Given the fact that their new secret agenda, *For Better or Worse*, was underway, Tabitha assumed the special meeting was related to it.

Well over a month and a half ago, Phoebe had proposed that in addition to discussing books, they take on a new mission—to catch the interest of the gentlemen for whom they held a secret *tendre*. She'd challenged them to perform a bold act to help the men who had caught their affection but had yet to return it, let alone notice them, to see them in a new light.

Phoebe had spoken with each of the league members privately, including Tabitha, and discovered that each of them had a man in their life they admired but who—to speak plainly—didn't know they existed even after several London Seasons.

Tabitha had come to believe that, as a wallflower, it was her fate to be ignored. She wasn't memorable or remarkable in any way. Her mother's poor health, whether true or feigned, meant Tabitha attended fewer and fewer events as she didn't like to leave her mother for long.

Phoebe viewed the futures of their members differently. Her impassioned call to action when she'd proposed the *For Better or Worse* agenda suggested they step into the light and do something out of the ordinary to catch the attention of the man they held in high esteem.

Phoebe would be the first to claim her curves were too generous and her features, along with brown hair and eyes, too plain. Tabitha, who had similar coloring but a slim figure that resembled a lad more than a full-grown woman, was envious of Phoebe's curves.

Tabitha's long legs and arms made her feel as if she'd never lost the gangliness of youth. She felt lanky and awkward much of the time. Unfortunately, the feeling intensified in social situations. Was it any wonder that few men asked her to dance or made any effort to further their acquaintance?

But here with the members of the literary league, she knew she belonged and could offer her opinion without worry. The group had become a haven where she could be her true self.

Phoebe cleared her throat, a subtle hint that she intended to call the meeting to order. "Thank you for coming to this emergency meeting of the Mayfair Literary League. Unfortunate circumstances have occurred, and I owe you an explanation."

One of the many reasons Tibby, as she was known by most of her friends, admired Phoebe was because of her courage. She wasn't afraid to speak her mind, even if some of her ideas were unconventional.

Thus far, Tibby had only managed to find that same bravery during literary meetings. Sharing her opinion on books wasn't so difficult in front of the league. They listened to what she had to say, sometimes agreeing and sometimes not.

The first time she'd been brave enough to state her view had been incredibly liberating. A feeling that her ever-narrowing world rarely provided.

Now she worried whether she spoke too plainly at times during their book discussions. Who knew that Lady Tabitha Malton could be so outspoken? The thought nearly made her smile.

She hoped that meant she was making progress and finding her voice, but that had yet to be tested outside of the league.

"Are you all right?" Lady Harriet Persimmons asked Phoebe, concern puckering her brow.

Before Phoebe could answer, Frances Melbourne shook her head. "This is my fault," she said in a trembling voice.

"Frances, that isn't true," Phoebe protested.

Frances held the gazes of the members. "The two of us were speaking at the Alexander Ball four nights ago about my potential bold act and were overheard."

"By whom?" Tibby asked.

"The Earl of Bolton, for one," Frances said.

Gasps met Frances' statement followed quickly by murmurs of concern. To think Phoebe's fiancé had heard their plan was shocking, indeed.

"A few others heard as well," Phoebe added. "I'm afraid our *For Better or Worse* agenda is now public knowledge."

Frances pressed a gloved hand to her mouth, her distress obvious. "If I hadn't been talking about it, you wouldn't have answered. Worst of all, I fear that I placed your betrothal in jeopardy."

Phoebe shook her head. "This isn't your fault. The agenda was my idea." She paused to look at each of them briefly. "I still stand by it. I would've preferred our agenda remain private, but what is so wrong with what we hope to do?"

"I agree." Tibby shared a sympathetic look with both Phoebe and Frances.

"As do I," Harriet said, and the others chimed in with agreement as well.

At the last meeting, Phoebe had asked for a volunteer to be the next to implement her move, and Tibby had raised her hand. The moment had shocked Tibby to her core. Taking chances was not who she was.

"I never would've thought to volunteer if not for you, Phoebe," Tibby added. Not that she had actually done anything as of yet. But she intended to be the next member to move forward. The commitment wasn't one she took lightly.

The return of her childhood friend, Captain Michael Shaw, to England's shores after ten years abroad in the British Army had been the catalyst for her volunteering.

She'd held a secret affection for Michael since her sixth year when he'd presented her with a frog, his finest possession at the time. Their fathers had been good friends before they'd both passed on, and their families still lived next to each other in London. Their country estates were near each other as well.

Michael had been her best friend. They'd been inseparable for many years. But when he'd gone to university—perhaps even before that—he'd slowly drifted away. However, they'd exchanged numerous letters during his time away, and she liked to think they'd come to know each other even better. But eventually those letters had stopped.

Of course, they'd spoken since his return home a month ago. Several times. The shadows in his eyes squeezed her heart, as did the distance that now stood between them.

Phoebe's actions had made Tibby wonder if she could do something to change that. At the very least, she was determined to try. If there was even the smallest chance she could help Michael see her in a new way *and* help to quiet his demons, she intended to take it.

Just as soon as she found the courage to do so.

"Was your earl quite upset?" Winifred asked, returning Tibby's thoughts to the conversation.

"Yes, he was." Phoebe shook her head. "Words failed me when I tried to explain. He compared the league's mission to a wager at White's."

"It's not the same thing at all," Millicent countered with a frown.

"No," Phoebe said. "But it *did* sound terrible when he framed it in that light."

"It truly did," Frances added, her expression sorrowful as she held Phoebe's gaze. "Everyone was staring. Including Lady Lucinda."

"Oh, no. She's such a notorious gossip."

"How awful!"

"Of all people." Tibby shifted in her chair, able to easily imagine Lady Lucinda wielding the information like a sword, stabbing holes in the confidence of the league members before they could move forward with their plans. The situation could turn into a disaster.

"It is concerning that she overheard," Phoebe agreed. "That is one of the reasons for an emergency meeting. I'm afraid we will be thought of differently now that people know of our agenda. You may want to reconsider whether you wish to proceed with your bold act. Perhaps you'll also need to reconsider your membership in the literary league."

"Surely not." Tibby frowned and glared at each of the other members, daring them to say they wanted to quit. The determination flooding her gave her strength, and it was a heady feeling. "I, for one, am proud to be a member."

"I can't imagine anything so drastic will be necessary," Harriet said, her expression thoughtful. "I would hazard a guess that a far more interesting event will occur in a week or two and no one will remember our little book group or our secret agenda."

"The league is so much more than either of those things." Tibby's gaze took in the members again. "You are all my dear friends. And friends stick together through thick and thin."

Phoebe drew a slow breath. "While I would agree, my mother has suggested that we disband."

"No." Tibby's mouth went dry at the thought. "That's a terrible idea." Where would she be without the group?

"Wouldn't disbanding be the same as admitting we did something wrong?" Winifred asked.

The conversation continued while Tibby's mind churned. The worry of losing the group was unbearable. Unthinkable, in fact. She needed them too much.

How could she move forward with her own daring move without their support?

Before an agreement could be reached, the door to the drawing room opened, revealing the Earl of Bolton. His startled gaze took in the members before holding on Phoebe.

The tender exchange that followed made Tibby's heart ache with longing. Bolton looked at Phoebe as if she was his whole world. Though it seemed impossible to consider that something similar might happen to her, she had to try. The time had come to take action and claim her chance.

Much like Phoebe, she didn't want to live with regret. To watch Michael from afar, wondering what if...

She need only find the right moment to share what she had in mind with Michael. Tibby pressed her hand to her stomach, wondering if she could find the courage to do it.

And if there was any chance he might agree to her plan.

Chapter One

One week later

Michael Shaw strode into the drawing room, unsurprised to find it empty. A glance out the window at the fine morning was all it took to determine where his mother would be—in the garden, tending her beloved roses.

He'd been home just over a month after being gone much of the past decade, serving in the 50th Regiment of the British Army. The last several years had been spent in New Zealand during the Land Wars. His final post had been a brief stay in Sydney, Australia.

Seeing so many parts of the world had been thrilling, from the Taj Mahal to the Himalayas to Victoria Falls. But military life was not easy. He had endured more than he'd thought himself capable of and much of that had left a mark on his soul, if not his body.

He was pleased to be home. Mostly.

Michael glanced around the room, still amazed by how little had changed in his absence. The house was the same. His mother and grandmother were certainly older but much the same. Even his rooms had remained untouched. In truth, the lack of change was disconcerting.

Especially since he wasn't the same person as the young man who'd left.

Michael shook off his dark thoughts, not wanting to dwell on what he'd survived during his years away.

The time had come to turn over a new leaf.

Make a fresh start.

Begin anew.

But doing what?

That answer had yet to come to him. He was accustomed to having a purpose and though his mother, grandmother, and older brother, Markus, insisted he take time to relax and enjoy life after his years of duty, having this much free time was driving him crazy.

As the second son, it had been a natural path for him to enter the military and one he'd welcomed. He never would've guessed that leaving behind his duties in the army would be quite so challenging. Military life was far from pleasurable, though perhaps small moments of those days had been.

The sense of purpose was what he'd appreciated the most. Knowing that what he did mattered.

Whereas at home, whether he rose from bed each day didn't. He was left rudderless on the rolling sea of life.

Michael scoffed at his ridiculous thoughts. He'd started a hobby, hadn't he?

Botany was something Markus, his now married brother, the Earl of Trafford, had suggested. Michael had thought it a promising idea, and his mother had been thrilled given her love of flowers and gardening.

It was too soon to determine whether he enjoyed the activity. For now, it held his interest.

He'd been poring through a copy of *Principles of Scientific Botany* that Markus had presented to him. At least the text gave him something to read in the middle of the night when sleep eluded him, as it so often did. There was still much to learn, and the experiments he was doing would take time to yield results.

Unfortunately, patience wasn't one of his strong suits. He hoped his new hobby might help him gain the virtue.

He walked quickly out of habit rather than need, which tended to startle the servants, and descended the stairs to the garden door and stepped out. The morning air was cool for June, but the blue sky hinted at warmer temperatures to come.

The sky was a different color abroad—sharper, deeper. London's blue always seemed to be coated in a sheen of grey, whether from the fog or the soot that plagued the city, was difficult to tell.

He walked along the curving paths and past precisely trimmed boxwood hedges until he found his mother settled near a bed of roses that she pruned. "Good morning, Mother."

Her beaming smile as she looked up at him from beneath the wide brim of her hat made him feel guilty. There was no denying how pleased the Dowager Countess of Trafford was to have him home. He was happy to be back as well.

It was just...

What? he wondered, not for the first time.

He was restless and often ill-tempered but couldn't precisely name the reason why.

"Michael." Her gaze raked over him as if to gauge his mood. That made him feel guiltier. "Good morning to you as well." She set down her shears and glanced around the garden. "Isn't it a lovely day?"

"It is." He could easily agree to that. Even more, he appreciated that she didn't ask how he was. The question tended to put him in a foul mood. "I wondered if you remembered the name of the rose you were admiring at the Hawkins' garden party last week."

"It was a tea rose, one with pointed blooms. The color was wonderful, was it not? A perfect blend of peach and pink."

"Indeed," Michael agreed. It had caught his eye as well. So classic and delicate yet full and lush. The fragrance had been especially appealing. "I thought I might try my hand at growing a version of them."

While there were only three main types of roses—old garden, modern garden, and wild roses—those could be divided into additional categories, very few of which he could remember. Perhaps that was a sign he'd chosen the wrong hobby.

His mother clasped her gloved hands together, her smile even brighter. "Oh, that would be lovely."

Her happiness alone made him want to try. To take a chance and risk failure on this small scale. He didn't like failing at anything, which had made him a fine officer. He wasn't certain if that same determination to succeed would serve him in civilian life.

"The color was especially appealing." She turned her head to study the deep red roses she'd been trimming. "I find I am no longer as enamored with these after seeing those tea roses."

Michael had to agree. The red roses looked like painted ladies on a street corner, trying too hard to call attention to themselves. He preferred a more subtle beauty, he supposed.

"Did you see your grandmother this morning?" she asked.

"Not yet. She wasn't in the drawing room when I passed by."

His grandmother preferred needlework to gardening and frequently warned her daughter-in-law of the hazards of too much time spent outdoors.

One of the reasons his mother liked having him home was to help keep an eye on his grandmother. She had declined in the past few years, being less active and often remaining home.

It was the cycle of life, he supposed. But that didn't keep his heart from aching at the idea of her eventually passing.

Watching his mother work in the garden made him pleased she had changed so little in his absence. She had always been a steadfast, loving presence in his life. He adored her, even when she continually hinted that he should find a wife. That happened more and more frequently of late.

Marriage was not on the near horizon as far as he was concerned. How could he consider marrying when he had yet to adjust to his return to England? Nor did he think he could find a bride who would put up with his poor moods.

Besides, there was no rush for him to marry if he chose to marry at all. Unfortunately, his mother and grandmother held a different opinion. His protests fell on deaf ears. Nor did they listen to his suggestion that he have a place of his own.

"You've only just arrived home," his mother had pleaded. "Let us enjoy your company for a few months before you leave us."

"I would only be a short distance away."

She scowled, making her opinion clear. "And we would never see you despite that. Don't tell me differently as your brother promised the same, and we rarely see him."

Michael knew that to be true. Markus and his wife had chosen to live elsewhere for a time before they eventually moved into the family home. Michael understood. Marriage would be an adjustment, one made more complicated with additional family members under the same roof.

"Besides, I don't think you should be alone right now. Not until you've had a chance to become accustomed to your return." The worry in her eyes made it clear that he hadn't hidden his restlessness as well as he'd hoped.

"Very well," he'd agreed. "For a few more weeks."

Most of the time, he enjoyed being home where he was spoiled by the two ladies in his life. They'd had the cook prepare his favorite meals and made certain he had every creature comfort he could possibly need.

Yet he could feel the urge to escape their smothering good intentions more and more often.

He'd reconnected with a few friends from his university days and attended an event or two when his mother insisted, but for the time being, he would rather stay home.

The house offered plenty of room for them all. His mother had offered a corner of the greenhouse that sat at the back of their property for him to use for his botany experiments. They'd installed a work table and shelves for his supplies as well.

The large garden offered space when he had the urge to be outside, which he often did. The area felt even bigger because their neighbor's garden ran alongside theirs, separated only by a wrought-iron fence and a few hedges rather than the high brick wall that edged the rest of their property.

He studied the well-tended Dunford garden through the fence, wondering what Tibby was doing at the moment. She and her mother had called soon after his return. He'd been pleased to see Tibby, though concerned about Lady Dunford, who seemed unwell. Or rather, she'd told him she'd been unwell.

She'd looked perfectly fine to him with a hint of color in her cheeks and a sturdy frame. The older lady didn't seem to be wasting away despite her remarks to the contrary.

He hadn't missed the tightening of Tibby's expression when Lady Dunford had described her most recent illness. Michael need only look at his own mother, who took pride in her good health, to understand how difficult it would be to live with someone who lamented about every ache and pain, whether real or imagined.

As if he'd conjured her from his thoughts, Tibby stepped out of the garden door with a basket in hand and wearing a wide-brimmed straw hat secured with a bow beneath her chin, seemingly unaware of their presence.

"I worry about her," his mother whispered as she also watched Tibby. "Lady Dunford seems determined to be ill. Each time I see her, her latest sickness is all she speaks of. That must be a challenge for Tabitha."

"I was thinking the same." Already, he'd noted how rarely Tibby left the house other than to spend time in their garden. Then again, perhaps she preferred to remain home, much as he did.

He knew that eventually, he'd return to an active life of some sort. But would Tibby have that chance?

"Does Lord Dunford call often?" he asked.

Victor, Tibby's older brother, had inherited the year after Michael's brother. Dunford had married two years ago but did not yet have children, according to Michael's mother. Much like Markus, Dunford and his wife chose to live elsewhere for now.

"Monthly. Perhaps more often at times." His mother shared a look with him. "Not often enough to truly help."

Michael grimaced. "I confess that I'm not certain how often I would call if you spoke only of your poor health."

"True. But where does that leave Tabitha?"

The Dunford garden was more practical than theirs, with a large kitchen garden set aside for growing vegetables and one of a similar size for herbs. They also had numerous flower beds but nothing like his mother's.

He'd noted Tibby working in the garden often, so he had to think its flourishing plants were owed to her efforts rather than solely to the gardener.

As if feeling the weight of their regard, Tibby looked up and met his gaze. Her immediate smile and friendly wave had him returning in kind.

She had changed little as well, though she was certainly more graceful than the gangly girl he remembered from childhood. Her lithe form and the elegant lift of her chin brought to mind a ballerina he'd watched perform in Paris during a brief stay several years ago.

He gave himself a mental shake at the odd comparison. Tibby was just Tibby. A long-time friend and next-door neighbor, nothing like an exotic ballet dancer.

Yet as he watched her walk to the herb garden and start her work, he realized that at least she had a purpose. Perhaps she was happy with her lot in life.

With a sigh, he bid his mother goodbye and strode toward the greenhouse to see if his botany experiments had wielded any results.

TIBBY WATCHED MICHAEL out of the corner of her eye, her smile fading when he departed soon after she emerged. Typical of the men in her life. First Michael, leaving for the army. Then her father, passing on. And finally, her brother when he'd left home and married soon after.

Which left her here, tending her mother and the garden. She huffed a breath of annoyance at the pitiful direction of her thoughts. It wasn't their fault that her world felt as if it were growing smaller.

What truly concerned her was Michael and the unhappiness he exuded. It seemed as if only part of him had returned home.

She'd been thrilled when Lady Trafford had first mentioned his expected return and beyond excited when she'd caught sight of him striding through the garden.

But those feelings had shifted to concern when she'd finally had the opportunity to welcome him home.

The man who'd returned was familiar but a stranger. Dear, yet distant. Michael, but a shadowed version.

Of course, he'd experienced events she couldn't imagine. But to see how much those had affected him was worrying. With one glance, she'd noted his restlessness. A hollowness that spoke of how much he'd been hurt—at least on the inside—by what he'd experienced.

Had he been hurt physically as well? At a glance, he looked much like himself. Perhaps a wiser, more mature version, but still Michael.

The flash of temper in his green eyes, the tightening of his lips, and the impatience in his body were signs he'd changed.

Never mind how much she longed to hear the details and try to help ease the burden he carried. He didn't want to talk about what he'd endured. Not to her, at any rate.

The few questions she'd asked during their brief visits had been met with vague answers and a dismissive smile that suggested she wouldn't understand.

The thought had her lifting her chin. She liked to think she would. At the very least, she was an excellent listener. That was more than most people could say.

She straightened her shoulders. If she was going to make her move, it needed to be soon. The idea she'd come up with was more than bold and would require courage to even suggest. She told herself she was waiting for the right opportunity to do so.

But could she? Would she?

Tibby heaved an exasperated sigh, clipped more lavender to add to her basket, along with two roses, and then stood.

It wasn't as if she could call out her plan through the fence. If she was patient, the right time would present itself.

She paused before the door, wondering whether that was true or if she was simply fooling herself. More than two weeks had passed since she'd raised her hand to volunteer at the Mayfair Literary League. Phoebe's wedding was in a few days.

Yet Tibby still had nothing to report. Would she have to confess to the group that she hadn't done anything at their next meeting?

Of course, her friends would still offer understanding and support. But how could she face them and say she'd done nothing to change her circumstances?

As Phoebe had confided in her, the idea of not taking action was nearly unbearable. Tibby simply had to do something before the next scheduled meeting.

Had to. Had to. Had to.

She repeated the words under her breath as she made her way inside and up the stairs to her mother's bedroom.

"Good morning, Mother." Tibby managed a bright smile, certain her mother wouldn't know the difference between a true one and a forced one. Not when she was so intent on herself and her latest supposed illness.

"Tabitha. I was wondering where you were." Her mother's brow furrowed, and her lips turned downward with displeasure.

Those small signs were both familiar and unwelcome. Today was not going to be a good day.

"I took a few minutes to clip these for you." Tibby showed her the beautiful roses and the fragrant lavender in her basket but didn't offer them when she knew they'd be refused.

"Oh. How nice. Could you have Alice warm my tea? It is too cold to enjoy."

"Of course." Tibby told herself not to be bothered by the response as it was what she'd expected. But that didn't completely remove the hurt the small rejection caused.

As the hours of each day passed, and her mother dealt one small rejection after another, they added up to a heavy burden.

Tibby rang the bell then spoke to the maid in the corridor, so Alice didn't have to endure more of her mother's complaints.

She returned to the bedroom and retrieved a vase from a nearby table. "I thought the flowers might cheer you since you haven't been feeling well." She studied her mother, unable to suppress the hope that one of these days, she'd return to the previous version of herself.

"Hmm." Her mother folded her arms over her stomach and stared out the window.

"Perhaps you'll feel up to sitting in the garden later," Tibby suggested.

"I doubt that, dear. I feel so terribly weak." Her mother pulled the covers tighter and leaned against the pillows. "So tired."

"I'm sorry. Perhaps rest is what you need." But that was all her mother did—rest.

Tibby feared the lack of activity would weaken her. However, she'd tried everything she could think of to convince her to attend events or take some exercise to no avail.

If she didn't want to rise from bed, there was little Tibby could do to convince her otherwise.

Only a visit from her son seemed to stir her from her bedroom. Unfortunately, those were few and far between. Her brother had little patience for their mother's illnesses, whether feigned or real, and quickly grew frustrated when he called.

How could Tibby blame him when she was running out of patience as well? It was ironic that the quality was something she was often praised for. If only everyone knew how little she had.

The thought made it even clearer that her idea for her *For Better or Worse* mission was an excellent one.

But could she convince Michael to agree? What if he did so only out of pity?

Desperate times called for desperate measures. She simply had to find the proper moment to move forward for the benefit of all involved, including Michael and her mother.

"How unfortunate that you're not feeling well," Tibby said. "I had hoped we could call on Lady Trafford tomorrow."

"Oh?" A flash of interest reflected in her mother's eyes. "Perhaps I will feel better by then."

"I hope so." Tibby's stomach tightened at the idea of speaking with Michael about her plan. But she had to do something. That meant finding the courage to proceed.

She'd practiced in the mirror and thought she had the right tone—casual, logical as if his answer didn't matter overmuch. She pressed a hand to her middle. Never mind that it mattered more than he could ever know.

Tomorrow was the day. *For Better or Worse*. What an apt description.

Chapter Two

The following morning, Michael rose early, which was no surprise given how fitfully he'd slept. Memories had taken over his dreams until it felt as if he couldn't remember what was true and what he'd only imagined.

Luckily, the fog cleared once he started his day.

He hurried down the stairs only to realize he'd startled Stokes, their long-time butler. With a sigh, he reminded himself to move more slowly. It wasn't as if he had somewhere to be.

"Good morning," he greeted Stokes, noting again that the elderly servant hadn't seemed to age at all. One more reminder of how much Michael had. "I'll be in the greenhouse if anyone needs me."

"Very well, Captain." Stokes gave what seemed like an encouraging nod. At least, that was how Michael was going to take it. He needed all the encouragement he could get. "Would you care for breakfast first?"

"I'll wait to eat with Grandmother." His grandmother was also an early riser and seemed to enjoy breaking her fast with him. His mother preferred a light meal in her room.

Michael continued to the greenhouse, drawing in the earthy fragrance and warm air the moment he opened the door of the building. The scent alone helped to soothe his senses, much like a warm blanket on a cold winter's day.

Unfortunately, the sensation didn't last nearly long enough based on what he'd experienced the last few weeks. The restlessness that plagued him would soon overcome the peaceful feeling, and he'd be striding out of the greenhouse door again in search of some other activity to calm his thoughts.

But he'd take what he could get of peace and be grateful for it. This morning, he was going to graft another rose by taking a piece from one plant and fusing it into another. Though it was early in the year to do so as mid-summer was when the plants were in full bloom and provided the best results, he still hoped for some success.

He cleaned the shears and knife he intended to work with, using a cloth and alcohol to do a proper job of it. Next, he pruned the rootstock plant to remove dead foliage.

After careful consideration, he selected a rose stem with numerous leaves, a sign of good health. He removed the thorns and a bud from the middle of the stem, doing his best to cut at a forty-five-degree angle to promote better circulation per the instructions he'd read in the book Markus had given him.

"Damn." The stab of pain to his forefinger suggested he hadn't been as careful with the knife as he thought. The small injury bled a surprising amount.

He uttered a second oath and set aside the knife to press a rag on the cut. The bleeding refused to subside until he finally tore a strip of fabric to bind it.

With less coordinated efforts because of the makeshift bandage, he cut an inch-long T into the exterior layer of rootstock between two nodes. The trick, according to what he'd read, was to be careful not to penetrate the cambium layer, which was a pale green color. During his previous attempts, he was certain he'd cut too deeply.

With that completed to his satisfaction, he cut off the top and bottom of the stem he would attach to the rootstock. It had a bud eye, and he cut into the stem deeply this time to penetrate the pale green layer. Taking care to make certain the bud eye faced upward, he inserted the small part into the larger plant. Then he checked his work, hoping this one would take.

Botany was interesting. More interesting than he'd originally anticipated. He enjoyed learning new things and grafting was certainly a way to challenge his mind.

He wished he could lose himself in the process of these experiments. As of yet, that hadn't happened.

After working a while longer, he tidied up the work table, rinsed his hands in the bucket of water that stood nearby, and returned to the house for breakfast.

His grandmother, Lady Anne Stannish, was a gem, and he thoroughly enjoyed spending time with her. She conducted herself with a regal air and was very opinionated, never hesitating to share her thoughts. Her snowy white hair and bright blue eyes added to her noble appearance. This morning, she wore a deep pink wrapper with a brown sash and matching wide cuffs.

Michael found her company entertaining. However, his mother often grew frustrated with her lack of diplomacy.

He believed that anyone who lived into their eightieth year could be as opinionated as they wanted. He hoped he had the same sharp wit and dry humor as his grandmother when he reached her age if he were so lucky.

"Michael." She looked him up and down then lifted a brow. "Where have you been so early this morning?"

"Working in the greenhouse." Saying that brought nearly as much satisfaction as doing it. He hated when he had to answer with 'Nothing.'

"And how did you find your time there?" She continued to look at him expectantly as if waiting for a true answer. Something with depth and meaning. If only he had an interesting response to share.

"I am attempting to create a new variety of roses," he said as he took a seat. "It is too soon to say for certain what the outcome will be, but I hope for good results."

"What kind of rose?" She glanced over her shoulder, and Stokes immediately retrieved the silver coffee pot from the sideboard to refill her cup.

"A tea rose like the peachy pink one we admired at the garden party. Do you remember it?" If he could create something like that, he would feel accomplished.

"Of course, I do." She frowned. "Do you think I have so little of my mind left?"

"Not at all. There were many beautiful flowers to admire, and I wasn't certain if those particular ones made as much of an impression on you as they did on me." He dug into his eggs and toast with the hope his answer had appeased her.

"Is your knife sharper than you expected?" Her gaze dropped to the strip of cloth he still had tied to his finger.

He should've removed it to avoid questions. "Something like that," he said with a smile.

"While working with sharp instruments one should keep their mind focused on the task at hand."

"You're right, Grandmother." Perhaps he didn't like her forthrightness as much as he thought. At least not when it was directed at him.

"What else do you have in store for the day?"

He focused on chewing his sausage as he tried to think of an answer that might satisfy her and himself. "A bit more work in the greenhouse. Perhaps a ride in the park as well."

"Hmm." Based on her doubtful expression that wasn't the answer she wanted.

He released a breath, realizing his agenda for the day didn't satisfy him either. But until he thought of a better way to spend his time, this would have to do.

What would happen when he finally moved to his own place? He wouldn't have a breakfast companion or a greenhouse at his disposal. How would he spend his time? The question was disconcerting.

He'd already realized that spending too much time alone often left him in low spirits. He supposed he did need more time to adjust to leaving the military's structured life than he cared to admit.

The rest of the morning passed slowly as Michael continued to work in the greenhouse. He paused briefly for luncheon then returned to his work in the afternoon.

He had decided grafting just one or two roses wasn't enough. At least that's what he told himself. He did another six and only managed to cut one other finger. The second injury made him wish he was better at this. Or better at something.

A knock on the door interrupted his dour thoughts. He turned to see Stokes in the doorway of the greenhouse.

"Pardon the interruption, sir, but Lady Trafford wanted you to know that Lady Dunford and Lady Tabitha have called. She would like you to join them for tea if you're available."

"Of course. I'll be there shortly." He couldn't deny the feeling of relief at having an excuse to step away from his work.

He tidied up the area, washed his hands, and retrieved his suit coat from where he'd left it on a peg, hoping he looked presentable, then made his way to the drawing room.

His gaze swept the room, holding on Tibby, pleasure filling him at her presence. Her brow puckered as she listened to his grandmother speak. He hoped she hadn't caused Tibby offense by something she said.

Tibby looked different today. Her gloved hands were tightly clasped in her lap, suggesting she was anything but relaxed. Her pale pink gown was quite becoming with her dark hair and a hint of rose in her cheeks. The matching hat she wore sat high on her head and its brim was decorated with small white rosebuds. Though she normally wore her hair in a neat chignon, today's version was looser with a few strands framing her face.

He frowned, thinking he much preferred it tidier. This style made him think of her as a woman rather than a long-time friend. Perhaps he didn't want change after all.

"MICHAEL!" LADY TRAFFORD exclaimed, startling Tibby from her musings. "How good of you to join us."

She glanced up to see Michael studying her with a rather perplexed look, making her wonder at his thoughts. His close regard made her even more nervous than she already was. Had he somehow guessed her intent?

No. Of course, he couldn't. How silly to think that. Her nerves were trying to get the better of her. Where was her courage when she needed it?

He continued to stare, causing her to shift in her seat. The anxiousness she'd been fighting all day grew worse, her stomach tightening with unease.

Michael moved closer, greeting her mother first and then her. "How kind of you to call," he said, the warmth in his green eyes that brought to mind the dark green of a deep forest suggesting he meant it.

"We thought it silly to continually wave through the fence when we live right next door," Tibby blurted even as heat climbed her cheeks. What a ridiculous statement. Everyone in the room knew they lived next door.

"I'm pleased you called." Michael's easy smile hinted at the carefree, jovial man he used to be and helped to calm her nerves.

This was Michael. Not a stranger. Of course, she would be able to suggest her plan. It would be to both their benefits.

She bit her lip. The problem was that there was more at stake for her. If she didn't have this deep, abiding affection for him, it would be simpler. His answer wouldn't matter as much.

And if he did agree, by some miracle, it was just the beginning. She still had to find a way to help him see her in a different light when they were together. To help him look at her as someone more than he used to know.

Good heavens. This was impossible.

"Isn't that right, Tibby?"

Her head jerked up from where she'd been staring at the brightly patterned rug to meet her mother's gaze, realizing she'd lost track of the conversation. "I'm sorry?"

Her mother frowned. "I was saying that you don't care to attend events as often as you used to."

Tibby hesitated. The issue was that her mother made it clear that she didn't like it when Tibby left her. However, Tibby had used that same excuse when friends inquired about whether they would see her at various functions.

It was easier to tell the lie than admit that her mother was manipulating her into staying home more and more often and that Tibby was allowing her to. The only functions she refused to miss were the literary league meetings.

"Perhaps attending a few more would be enjoyable," Tibby said, careful to avoid looking at her mother.

"I'm trying to convince Michael to attend some as well." Lady Trafford smiled at her son. "It would provide an opportunity to meet eligible young ladies."

Michael's mother had said something similar during their last visit. Tibby noted that he didn't return his mother's smile. That gave her hope. She had to think that meant he wasn't in a hurry to find a wife, despite Lady Trafford's prodding.

Watching Michael interact with his mother and grandmother made her admire him even more. He obviously loved them both dearly and was gentle and respectful when he responded to what they said.

He had settled into a wingback chair, slouching slightly. His dark hair was brushed to the side though a few tendrils were out of place as if he'd recently run his hands through it.

She sighed, easily imagining doing the same.

His broad shoulders filled out his brown suit coat so well. His muscled thighs were apparent beneath the tightly pulled fabric of his trousers. While she'd seen him in states of half-dress when they were young, that had been over a decade ago. What might he look like now? With those narrow hips and flat stomach, she could almost imagine his sculpted physique.

She blew out a breath as her vivid imagination took hold.

A bit of dirt smudged one sleeve. He must've been working in the greenhouse again. What was he doing for so many hours in there? He'd never been particularly fond of gardening before. Had he developed a passion for it while abroad?

He ran a hand along his thigh, and she caught sight of strips of cloth tied to two fingers. Clearly, he'd hurt himself. She'd done her share of that in the garden. One wrong move with the sharp shears was all it took.

"Lady Tabitha?"

Her breath caught as her gaze swung to meet his mother's. She paused a moment, hoping to remember part of the conversation. But she hadn't heard any of it. "I beg your pardon. I confess that I was woolgathering."

"Not at all." Lady Trafford dismissed her concern with the wave of two elegant fingers. "I was asking how your herb garden was coming along."

"Quite well, thank you. The weather has been assisting my progress. I assume it has yours as well, for your flowers look especially beautiful already."

"Why herbs?" Michael asked to her surprise.

"I do enjoy flowers, and we grow quite a few." She glanced at her mother as Tibby's preference to grow plants that were practical rather than pretty often caused a disagreement between them. "I suppose I like nurturing plants that serve a purpose. We have an herb garden along with a kitchen garden for vegetables. Of course, some of those flowers are very pretty."

"Nonsense." Lady Stannish slapped a hand on the arm of her chair. "You can't cut those to display in a vase like you can roses."

"Exactly." Tibby's mother straightened as she gave a single nod of agreement and cast a meaningful glare at Tibby. Never mind that when Tibby cut flowers for her mother, she ignored them. "That is what I keep saying."

"I, for one, appreciate that you like plants with a purpose." Michael's smile started in his eyes before finding his lips.

Tibby's stomach fluttered for an entirely different reason than when they'd arrived. Did he have any idea how handsome he was?

His attraction made it all the more imperative that she act before he started attending events. The eligible ladies would swarm on him like bees on clover.

Once that happened, he'd never see Tibby. She didn't stand out in a crowd. Having endured five Seasons amidst the *ton* with little success left her no doubt of that. With each year that passed, she took a step closer to the spinster shelf.

It wasn't until Phoebe had asked the literary league if they were prepared to live always wondering "what if" that Tibby had considered trying to change her current path.

She loved her mother and didn't mind watching over her. But not to the exclusion of all else—not to the exclusion of having a chance at love and a family of her own.

The spear of longing that shot through her at the heady thought stole her breath. To have Michael look at her each day as he just had allowed a tiny bud of hope to bloom within her.

What if...

"What do you do with all those herbs?" Apparently, Lady Stannish wasn't finished with the topic.

Tibby turned her thoughts to the question. "We use them for cooking and cleaning as well as for medicinal purposes. Nothing goes to waste." Tibby liked being resourceful and had taken it upon herself to learn as much as she could about not only growing herbs but using them. "Our cook is quite knowledgeable and sparked my interest in such things."

Michael nodded.

Tibby hoped it was as much in approval as in understanding. She rarely received support or appreciation for her interests. Certainly not from her mother.

The conversation moved on and soon tea was over.

Unfortunately, not once did she have a chance to speak privately with Michael.

Panic set in when they stood to take their leave. She tried desperately to think of a reason to have a moment alone with him.

She held back as her mother said goodbye and started toward the doorway until at last, she looked at Tibby. "Aren't you coming?"

"Yes, of course." Tibby rushed forward, nearly tripping in her haste.

Michael reached for her arm to ensure she had her balance.

While she'd wanted a moment with him, this wasn't what she'd had in mind. She managed a smile, hoping her face wasn't overly red with embarrassment.

He kept hold of her arm, his brow crinkling as he looked at her. "Is all well?"

"Yes, of course. Why?"

He glanced to where her mother now stood just out of the drawing room, along with his mother and grandmother, leaving them almost alone. "You seem rather out of sorts today."

"I do?" Her heart pounded painfully.

This was her chance. Perhaps the only one she would have.

She opened her lips, yearning filling every cell in her body as she looked into his eyes.

Then her mother's voice came clearly from the doorway. "I don't know what I'd do without Tabitha. She takes such good care of me."

She clamped her lips tight as guilt settled like a bag of potatoes on her shoulders, heavy and unwelcome. She couldn't do it. Her gaze fell to where he held her arm, the makeshift bandage visible. "I'm sorry you're hurt."

With courage she wished she could've used differently, she took his hand and held it with her gloved ones. Calluses were visible on his fingers and palm, making her wonder what he'd done during his time in the army.

She wished her hands were bare so she could touch those rough places. Then her gaze lifted to meet his.

He was different than he used to be. But every so often, she caught glimpses of the person he used to be. The one she knew so well.

What if…

Tibby drew a breath and opened her mouth again. But nothing came out. She quickly closed it, dropped his hand, and then stepped away. "I had better join Mother."

She hurried out of the room, cursing her lack of courage. This was for the best, she told herself. He would've said no. More than likely, he would've laughed at her suggestion.

Her shoulders sank as she realized she would have to tell the league members she'd failed. They'd be disappointed, but not nearly as much as she was disappointed in herself.

Chapter Three

"Where are you going?" Tibby's mother asked.

Tibby looked up as she put on her shawl, surprised to see her mother standing in the doorway of her bedroom. Tibby suppressed a groan.

It had taken all night to work up the courage to decide to make another attempt to speak with Michael. To have her mother question her only made the task seem more impossible. Especially after what Tibby had overheard her telling Lady Trafford yesterday.

I don't know what I'd do without Tibby.

But her plan would benefit her mother as much as herself. It wasn't healthy for either of them that her mother was so dependent on Tibby.

She'd turned the options over and over during the night and realized she had to try. Living with regret wasn't an option.

Michael might actually agree to her plan and begin to see her in a new light, just as Phoebe's earl had.

If Tibby did nothing and Michael was soon courting someone else, she couldn't bear it. That was enough to have her rise with purpose this morning.

She searched for an answer to her mother's question, but nothing came readily to mind. She was terrible at lying. A portion of the truth would have to do. "Michael has a few cuts on his hand, so I am taking him some of our salve."

The fact that her mother was out of bed this early came as a surprise. She rarely left her room until mid-morning. Why did she have to change the pattern today?

The loose grey wrapper with cream-colored lace she wore suggested she was up for the day. Her dark hair had faded, and touches of white marked her temples, clearly visible due to the tight knot in which it was bound.

"He won't want your ointment." The discouraging frown on her mother's face sent Tibby's heart sinking once again. Why did it feel as if her mother referred to her rather than the ointment?

He won't want you.

Hadn't that same worry circled her thoughts as she'd prepared for her errand?

"He might." Tibby lifted her chin and repeated that to herself. *He might want her.* It was a chance she had to take. Before it was too late. "I will offer it anyway. It's the neighborly thing to do."

Her mother's lips twisted with familiar disapproval.

Tibby was used to condemnation since she received it every time she left the house for any reason. That wasn't going to stop her this morning. The only thing that might was her agitated stomach.

"Don't stay too long," her mother said, her frown still in place. "I'm certain we wore out our welcome yesterday."

"I thought you enjoyed visiting with Lady Trafford and Lady Stannish. Has that changed?"

"I suppose I did. However, I'm sure they have other callers today." Her mother's tone almost seemed to suggest she was envious. But she'd turned away friends so often that now they rarely called. "Isn't it too early for visiting?"

"We are friends and neighbors. Surely the rules don't apply." Tibby pulled on her gloves then reached for the small tin of ointment she'd prepared using yarrow. "I will be back directly." She kissed her mother's cheek as she passed by.

Then she marched down the stairs and out the door, fearing that if she slowed her pace she might turn around.

She had already rehearsed what to say and hoped she could remember it. She knocked on the front door, relieved their familiarity meant she needn't bother bringing a maid.

Stokes, the butler, opened the door and smiled. "Good morning, Lady Tabitha." He gestured for her to come inside. "To what do we owe the honor of this visit?"

She held up the small tin of salve, grateful for the excuse it gave her. "I would like to give this to Captain Shaw if he's available. I noted yesterday that he had several cuts and thought this might help."

"How kind of you. I believe he's in the greenhouse again this morning." The butler led the way toward the back of the house.

With each step, Tibby's heartbeat sped. She pressed a hand to her chest and drew in a deep breath, hoping to calm herself before she had a seizure or the like. Perhaps she should've simply checked the greenhouse before knocking on the front door.

"He has been spending a lot of time out there since his return." Tibby didn't know what made her say that when Stokes already knew it.

"I do believe he prefers to keep busy." Stokes paused at the back door and gestured for her to precede him. "I'm certain he'll be happy to see you." He nodded and remained in place.

Relief filled her at the realization that she wouldn't have to speak with Michael in front of Stokes. She hated to imagine what he might think if he heard her.

The path to the greenhouse was short, and she soon opened the door, greeted by the familiar scent of plants, soil, and moist air. The aisles were narrow, packed with pots of plants in various stages of growth as well as gardening supplies. The sound of someone muttering drew her toward the back of the greenhouse.

Michael stood before a work table, his suit coat removed, and his shirt sleeves rolled up. The sight of his muscled forearms covered with dark hair sent tingles along her skin.

He didn't look up at her approach, so she took a moment to simply admire him. His dark hair was mussed, and a smudge of dirt marked his cheek. Various pieces of stems lay strewn across the table along with several pots of dirt.

She slowly approached as memories filled her. This man had remnants of the boy who had presented her with a frog but was more like the young man with whom she had walked through fields during summers in the country.

Times had been much simpler then.

Unable to resist, Tibby drew closer still to look around his shoulder, curious to see what he was doing. "Grafting roses?"

He jerked, making it clear he hadn't heard her. She pressed a gloved hand on that tanned masculine forearm to reassure him. "I'm sorry. I didn't mean to startle you."

"Tibby." His gaze raked over her face before it fell to where she touched him.

She quickly removed her hand, realizing how forward the gesture was. Never mind that she wished she could pull off her glove and touch him again. She longed to feel the same connection that she'd had before he'd left for the army.

Unfortunately, she didn't know if that was possible. They were both different people now.

"What brings you by this morning?" A smile played about his lips, suggesting he was pleased about something. Was the work going to his satisfaction or was he happy to see her?

Either way, she would much rather see the smile than the furrowed brow he'd worn so often since his return.

She closed her eyes briefly and gripped the tin as if her life depended on it. This was her chance.

Could she do it?

"I made some ointment for you." She shook her head, frustrated that the words weren't coming out correctly. "I mean I made the salve, and I thought it might aid your injuries."

He took the offered tin and looked at it with wonder followed by a broader smile. "So you're saying you made it, but not for me."

She recognized the teasing note in his voice but couldn't keep from defending herself. "I didn't make it for anyone in particular. I just—"

Michael chuckled. "I'm sorry. I couldn't resist teasing you."

There was that smile again. The one that caused her stomach to dip as if she'd taken an unexpected step off a cliff.

Maybe she had.

Suddenly she realized her plan would be more difficult than she had thought. If for some unknown reason Michael agreed, how was she ever going to hide her feelings for him?

Before she could respond, a stem he had just connected to a larger plant in a pot came apart, dropping to the table.

"Blast it." His wrinkled brow returned as he retrieved the short piece. "These never seem to want to stay together. I have yet to determine what I'm doing wrong." He spun the stem between his fingers, staring at it as if it might reveal answers.

"I'm sorry to say that I have no experience with grafting. I wish I could help."

"I reviewed the instructions again last night, and it seems fairly simple. But executing my plan is not."

Tibby couldn't help but smile. That was something to which she could relate. "Execution is often a challenge." She studied his profile. "You never liked to garden in the past. May I ask why you're doing this now? To what end?"

He looked at her in surprise. "For my mother. I would like to make a rose similar to one she admired at a garden party we attended."

"Hmm." While admirable, it didn't seem like enough motivation for the effort he was putting into it.

"What does that mean?" he asked with narrowed eyes.

"It's very kind of you." Tibby glanced around the greenhouse before meeting his gaze again. "But is all this making you happy?"

"Occasionally." He huffed out a breath. "That's not the point."

"It should be. You need to do something you feel passionate about." She removed her gloves then took the tin and opened the lid as she spoke. It was much easier to have this conversation while performing a task. "Something that you can't wait to return to each day." She dabbed a finger in the ointment and reached for his hand which bore another fresh cut. With a gentle touch, she placed the salve on each of the injuries then looked up at him again. "Something that drives you."

Michael stared at her with questions in his moss-green eyes as if she spoke a foreign language. As if he didn't know her as well as he thought he did.

The thought sent her stomach dancing.

That was the purpose of the *For Better or Worse* agenda. To help the man who held their affection to see them differently.

Though tempted to let it go at that and hope that what she'd said might be enough to help him truly see her, the brief moment wasn't enough.

She'd only be letting down herself, as well as the other league members. Boldness was required, and that was what she'd promised herself.

"The salve isn't the only reason I wanted to speak with you." Hoping her fingers weren't trembling, she released his hand, replaced the lid on the tin, and then set it on the table. "I would like to know if you'd consider assisting me with something."

"Of course."

She nearly smiled at his easy agreement, even if she couldn't bring herself to meet his eyes. "As you may have noticed, my mother often feels ill. However, she isn't. Ill, that is." Heat stung her cheeks as embarrassment took hold again. "She is unhappy. Remaining home and encouraging me to do so as well isn't going to change that."

"Tibby, I—"

She held up a single finger to hold off whatever he was going to say. She had to finish this before she lost her courage. "I couldn't help but notice your mother mentioning that you should look for a wife."

He scoffed. "She is far too focused on the topic."

"I might have a solution for us both." She swallowed hard, staring at the small expanse of skin visible above his loosened neckcloth and trying to pretend she was merely saying this before the mirror again. That bronzed skin only made her mouth drier. "What if we agree to a pretend betrothal?"

The words rushed out even as her heart rattled in her chest as if it wanted to flee the scene. So did she.

Still, she pressed onward. "I would like to encourage my mother to look at her future in a new way rather than relying on me to remain at her side for the rest of her days. My suggestion would also quiet your mother's reminders that you should marry. At least, until you're ready to do so."

"A pretend betrothal?" His befuddled expression hinted that he had no idea of what she was speaking.

She ignored that in favor of moving on to the details. "We could agree on a length of time. Perhaps three months. Maybe even six." She lifted one shoulder, uncertain how long would be best.

Long enough for him to realize he loved her. How long would that take?

What if he never did? Her chest tightened painfully at the worry.

"During our betrothal," she continued, willing him to remain silent for just another moment or two, "you would have time to decide what you want to do with your future without being pressed to find a wife. And I would have time to ease Mother back into the world."

She risked another glance at him, only to find him staring at her as if she'd lost her wits.

Dear heaven, she probably had. But it was too late to worry about that now. She jerked her gaze away, determined to keep going before her dwindling courage fled completely.

"At the end of that period, we will part ways with each of us having gained what we wanted." Except if they parted, she wouldn't have him. She would've lost everything, including his friendship most likely. Was her plan truly worth the risk?

"Tibby."

She glanced at him again and saw the answer written clearly on his face.

No. Most likely, *Hell, no.* And, *Are you mad?* for good measure.

Her breath caught. She couldn't bear hearing any of that. Not now at any rate. Managing to state her suggestion was as much as she could endure for now.

"I only ask you to consider it," she quickly added. "This could be the solution we both need." She tapped a finger on the tin. "Apply the salve twice more, preferably before bed."

The image of him preparing for bed had her blinking rapidly in an effort to clear it. Yet her physical reaction to the thought only confirmed her attraction to this man. She'd never had such thoughts about other men she'd met over the years.

"Do you have something in your eye?" he asked with a note of concern.

"No. I'm fine." She managed a smile and forced herself to stop blinking. "I must be going. Mother will wonder what's kept me. Enjoy your day."

Then she bolted as fast as her feet could carry her, leaving her gloves behind in her haste.

MICHAEL PACED THE GREENHOUSE for the next hour, his thoughts in turmoil even as he avoided looking at Tibby's gloves.

A pretend betrothal?

What on earth was she thinking? She was like a sister to him.

But wait. His mind rebelled at the lie. Those moments when she'd been speaking to him about finding passion while putting the ointment on his hand had made him feel anything but brotherly.

If not brotherly, then what?

He waved his hand in the air to dismiss the question only to knock over a clay pot and send it crashing to the floor.

"Damn." He bent to clean up the mess, his thoughts still reeling.

He was a man, wasn't he? A red-blooded man with...needs. And she...

Well, she was a woman, obviously. It wasn't as if he hadn't noted that. She was also attractive, he supposed.

He paused while picking up the broken pieces as he considered that further. Yes, she was nice enough to look at. Smooth skin, wide eyes the color of melted chocolate in a heart-shaped face. Her dark hair was rich in color. Her long limbs and slim hips might have stirred him once or twice since his return home.

In truth, he hadn't been able to keep from comparing her to the ballerina once the thought had come to mind. Especially in the dark of night.

None of that mattered. He shook his head and returned to cleaning up the mess. He and Tibby couldn't possibly become betrothed.

While he was growing weary of his mother's not-so-subtle remarks about marrying, that didn't mean he was prepared to act. She would get the hint soon enough. If she didn't, he would simply tell her again that he wasn't ready. While doing so might hurt her feelings, she'd understand.

He tidied up his work area, deciding he'd had enough of the greenhouse for now. His decision to stop for the day had nothing to do with the scent of lavender still lingering in the air. That smell more than likely came from one of the roses.

As quickly as possible, he strode out the door, only to return for the gloves and the ointment. He stuffed them in a pocket and then went into the house, more than ready to forget Tibby and her suggestion.

He entered the drawing room. "Good morning, Mother."

"And to you, dear. Have you been in the greenhouse again?"

"Yes." He glanced at the cuts on his fingers, noting they already felt better and no longer stung. But he didn't mention the ointment tin and gloves in his pocket or Tibby's visit to his mother. Somehow, it seemed like a poor idea.

"I'm so pleased you've found a hobby you enjoy."

"Hmm."

Tibby's words returned to him. She had a point. He didn't have a passion for botany. It was somewhat interesting, and he would like to create a rose for his mother. But that was the extent of his interest. He couldn't seem to get grafting right, nor could he repeat the names of various roses to save his life.

If he didn't continue with botany, how would he spend his days? Should he seek an occupation of some sort? The question was certainly worth consideration, especially given his limited finances.

"What else do you have planned in the coming days?" She lifted a brow, the picture of innocence.

He knew better. That look boded ill. He considered possible answers, but none came readily to mind. He didn't want to lie. "Difficult to say." Perhaps that would satisfy her.

He should've known better.

"We received an invitation to the Willaby Ball for tomorrow evening. It should prove to be a wonderful event."

"Oh? That's nice." He moved to the window, feigning interest in the street below.

"I have it on good authority that Lady Sophia Barnaby will be there."

"Who is she?" He wracked his memory but came up with nothing.

"A lovely young lady I would like you to meet." His mother paused for dramatic effect. "I think she could be the one."

"The one for what?" He turned back to look at her, knowing what she'd say but refusing to play along. Hadn't he already made it clear he wasn't ready to consider marriage?

"For a wife." Her smile was overly bright. "She could be perfect for you."

"Considering the fact that we've never met, I highly doubt it." Tibby's proposal returned to mind, not that it had ever left, and was suddenly more appealing.

"She is a beauty and comes from a good family. Her mother and I are dear friends," she continued as if he hadn't spoken. "Rumors are that her dowry is significant."

"Oh?" He stared out the window at Tibby's house while wondering what other qualities his mother would use to entice him.

"I only ask that you meet her. She is delightful."

"Have you spent any length of time with her?"

"Well, not really. But our brief encounters have been very enlightening."

He turned from the window to look at her, curious as to what would make a young lady "enlightening." "How so?"

"Well..." His mother seemed to realize she might have gone too far with her claim.

He took several steps closer. "Mother, as I have mentioned before, I'm not ready to consider marriage. Nor am I looking for a wife any time soon."

"Of course, dear." She waved her hand. "But what is the harm in looking? Meeting new friends is the first step."

"I don't want to take a step. Not in that direction."

"Michael." The pleading expression on her face nearly did him in. "I only want you to be happy. It is clear to me that you're not."

He ran a hand through his hair, disappointed that he hadn't managed to hide his restlessness. "It's not that I'm unhappy."

"But?" She lifted a brow.

"As we've discussed, it will take time for me to readjust to life in London." He swung away only to face her again, wanting to explain so she'd understand. "Life is much different here than what I am used to. For ten years, my days were filled with duties and responsibilities from dawn to dusk." He lifted a hand only to let it fall. "Here, there is little to do."

"You should relax after all you've endured."

"I'm not sure that's possible. Not yet." He shook his head. "Thinking of the future is more than I'm prepared to do right now." Especially when he didn't know how he wanted to spend tomorrow let alone the empty months that stretched ahead. As a second son, he had a limited income. He'd need to find a career of some sort eventually, especially once he moved to a place of his own.

"I understand. Truly. But what better way to pass the time than to meet people your age?"

Tibby's pretend betrothal was sounding better and better. He hated the feeling of disappointing his mother and didn't care for the pressure she unwittingly placed on him.

"Even your grandmother was impressed by Lady Sophia."

He smothered a groan. At the first opportunity, he needed to speak with Tibby and tell her that his answer was yes.

Definitely yes.

Chapter Four

Definitely no. His answer to Tibby was going to be no. That had become clear during the remainder of the day and into the night as he mulled over the possibility.

Tibby was a dear friend, and he refused to risk her reputation by agreeing to the crazy scheme of a pretend betrothal.

She'd made it sound logical at the time, and his mother pressing him to meet potential brides had tipped the scale.

Further consideration made it clear it wouldn't work.

He and Tibby would have to be convincing to make their families believe they had suddenly developed feelings for one another. That meant showing affection before they announced a betrothal.

Spending time with her would certainly be no hardship, but pretending to be smitten or perhaps even kissing her? He had difficulty wrapping his mind around those details, partly because thinking of them made him feel guilty as if he were betraying their friendship.

Those issues were only a portion of the problem. What would happen when they were ready to call an end to it? Obviously, Tibby would have to break off the betrothal. If Michael did, no other man would look twice at her. When she did so, what would happen to her reputation? She might not face total ruin, but a broken betrothal would certainly leave a stain.

No. It wouldn't work. Tibby deserved a man who cared for her as more than a friend and would stand by her side in the way a woman as special as she deserved. A man—the right man—who would be her partner for life.

Of course, he cared for Tibby. But his feelings were not passionate in nature.

Michael closed his eyes as a voice somewhere deep inside him protested. A voice he quickly smothered. Never mind that he couldn't name one man who was deserving of Lady Tabitha Malton.

He had never been one to take the easy path. Becoming betrothed to Tibby simply to keep his mother from suggesting he meet eligible young ladies was just that. Too easy.

He'd explained his feelings to his mother and hoped she'd honor his request to give him time. The coming days would show whether she had listened.

In the meantime, he owed Tibby an answer.

He rose from the chair in his father's old study where he'd been reading and looked out the window into the garden. The cloudy day had kept his mother inside, but he kept watching to see if Tibby was working in her garden.

Twice already today, he'd just missed her. She'd returned inside as he'd stepped out to speak with her. Could she be avoiding him?

To his relief, he saw her working in the herb garden again.

Perfect. He wanted the conversation over and done. Speaking to her in the garden would provide the privacy needed to allow him to explain. He planned to advise her that he appreciated her offer but couldn't possibly accept. While he wanted to help her, feigning a betrothal wasn't the right way to go about it.

He hoped she'd understand.

This time, he had no intention of missing her. He strode out of the study to the door at the end of the corridor and out to the garden.

To his dismay, Tibby rose and with nothing more than her usual wave, returned inside before he could make it clear he wished to speak with her.

That made three times that he'd missed her. Perhaps she'd changed her mind and realized how crazy her suggestion had been and that it would never work.

He ignored the disappointment that nudged him. If that were the case, it was for the best. His fingers found his pocket and slid along the soft gloves, which he'd intended to return to her. Odd, but the smooth fabric calmed him each time he touched it. Maybe he wouldn't return them to her yet.

But he still needed to speak with her. Now he'd have to wait until another opportunity presented itself.

He returned inside, debating whether to simply walk over and knock on her door. But if her mother caught wind of his arrival, she might read more into it. That might cause problems for Tibby.

"Is there something you need assistance with, Captain?" Stokes asked as he came upon Michael standing near the door.

"I was hoping to catch Lady Tabitha in the garden so I might have a word with her."

"I see. Would you care to have a message delivered?"

"No need." He preferred to keep the conversation casual. Putting it in writing made it more formal than he wanted. "It seems unlikely that she'll attend the Willaby Ball this evening," he muttered.

"I'd be happy to ask Henry if he knows," Stokes offered.

"The footman?" Michael asked. "How would he know?"

Stokes leaned close. "He's been friendly with Lady Tabitha's maid these last few weeks," he said in a low voice with a twinkle in his eye.

"Oh?"

"Wouldn't surprise me a bit if something came of it. They seem quite enamored with one another. Not that you heard it from me." The butler frowned. "Though I don't think Lady Trafford would disapprove."

"Nor do I." His mother treated the servants with more respect than most other ladies. She didn't take issue with them living their lives as long as they fulfilled their duties.

At any rate, Michael would welcome assistance from whoever could provide it, including the footman. "Please see if Henry has anything to share on the topic."

In short order, the footman knocked on the study and advised him that Lady Tabitha was going to the ball, the first one she'd attended this Season. She'd be going with a friend and the friend's mother. Lady Dunford would remain home, according to their maid.

Michael thanked Henry for the information. As the footman departed, he couldn't help wondering what his fellow army officers would think of him making plans based on servants' gossip. Then again, perhaps they'd approve of him using whatever means necessary to learn what he wanted to know.

The remainder of the day crawled by as he debated the best way to share his answer with Tibby. He was still undecided by the time they were preparing to depart for the ball.

Even his grandmother was joining them this evening, though Michael wondered if that was because she hoped to see his reaction to meeting Lady Sophia. He thought he'd made it clear to his mother that he didn't care to meet any ladies but based on his grandmother's secretive smile, he doubted his success.

Despite that concern, he had to admit he looked forward to seeing old friends he had yet to reach out to since his return home.

His mother's pride and happiness at his escort also couldn't be denied. He enjoyed seeing her smile. But he wasn't about to marry because of that.

After greeting Lord and Lady Willaby, they entered the ballroom. Michael was content to remain near his mother and grandmother for the time being. But he searched the crowd for Tibby, hoping to see her.

His gaze caught on someone who looked faintly like her. But she was some distance away and other guests continually blocked his view.

No. That couldn't be her. The lady's gown was a deep rose satin with pink and white striped ruffles around the low neckline and hem. Short puffs of sleeves left her upper arms bare above her white gloves. Her dark hair was swept up in an intricate fashion with twists and braids which elongated her neck.

His breath caught, his entire body stiffening as she turned, revealing her profile. Tibby had definitely changed since their youth.

She was beautiful. Intriguing. Elegant.

Her cheeks held a hint of color, whether from excitement or the warmth of the ballroom, he didn't know.

Before he could approach her, someone called his name. He turned to see Viscount Comfrey approaching. "Shaw. I didn't realize you were back. Taking a break from military life?"

"A permanent one." Michael reached out to shake the man's hand. "Good to see you, Comfrey. I hope you are well."

"Well enough, I suppose." He glanced around the room, his dissatisfaction obvious. "I'm sure you have noticed that little has changed in your absence. Same ballrooms. Same people."

"Perhaps some. But not all." Michael followed his gaze around the room and noted more unfamiliar faces than he expected. Once again, he found Tibby. That was one area that was turning out to be quite unexpected.

"When can we meet so you can tell me about your adventures?" Comfrey asked.

"I wouldn't want to bore you. Military life is not exactly exciting most of the time."

"Yes, but it is those bouts of excitement that make it worthwhile, right?"

Michael smiled but didn't correct him. Those moments were when fear and adrenaline waged war inside one. Where courage was tested and often wavered.

"I am eager to hear your stories since father refused to allow me to step foot off English soil other than a few uneventful trips abroad," Comfrey added.

"I'm sure they were far from boring knowing you."

"We did manage to have some amusing moments," Comfrey admitted with a grin. "So much so that now my mother is certain I need to marry post haste."

"I'm relieved to hear that I'm not the only one whose mother thinks my life will not be complete until I take a wife." Michael glanced to where she stood a short distance away. Luckily, she hadn't heard anything he'd said.

"I have no wish to rush into matrimony." Comfrey shook his head. "Being saddled with one woman for the rest of my life is bad enough. No need to jump into it any sooner than necessary."

They spoke for several more minutes before agreeing to meet at the club soon.

Michael advised his mother that he saw someone he wanted to speak with and eagerly moved to where Tibby had stood. Again, his progress was slowed when several friends from his university days greeted him as he passed. Some he was eager to renew his acquaintance with but not all. He hoped to be more selective in his friendships now.

Throughout the conversations, his gaze continually sought Tibby, who spoke with friends. They must be close as her expression grew animated at times. She wasn't dancing, much to his surprise, but was obviously enjoying herself.

No wonder she was weary of staying home with her mother so often. She deserved to have more freedom and not be burdened with her mother's care. Especially when Lady Dunford wasn't truly ill.

After bidding another acquaintance goodbye, Michael walked directly toward her, unwilling to wait to speak to her any longer. Her back was toward him, the smooth creaminess of her bare shoulder a distracting temptation—one he hadn't expected.

Should he reconsider her suggestion? He cared deeply for her and wanted to see her happy. If pretending to be betrothed would grant her that, didn't he owe it to her to aid her?

He was beginning to think his answer was definitely yes.

A SHIVER RAN ALONG Tibby's back, bringing with it a sudden awareness. She didn't have to look to know who was approaching.

Drat.

She should have found out if Michael was attending the ball this evening. She hadn't expected him to, based on their previous conversations. Perhaps his mother had talked him into it after all.

Each time she'd seen him earlier in the day, it had been clear that he wanted to speak with her. While it might have been childish to avoid him, she had wanted a little more time to come to terms with what she knew his answer would be. Was it so wrong to want to hold on to her dream for a little while longer?

Harriet, a friend from the literary league, tugged at the lace edging her high-necked gown while sending Tibby a questioning look. Why Harriet always wore that style when evening gowns normally had a much lower decolletage was a puzzle, especially when she seemed uncomfortable in them.

Tibby sighed and reluctantly turned to find Michael striding toward her with that quick pace of his. One that said he had a purpose.

As if *she* were his purpose.

Her heart squeezed at how handsome he looked in his evening attire. His hair was neatly brushed to the side and no smudges of dirt were visible anywhere. She rather missed them.

"Captain Shaw. What a pleasure to see you." She thought it best to keep the greeting formal. "May I introduce you to some friends of mine?"

"The pleasure would be mine," he said with a bow.

Tibby introduced Harriet, Frances, and Winifred. All three of her friends watched Michael with fascination. They appeared to think him as handsome as she did. She couldn't help the proprietary feeling that came over her, making her wish she could link her arm through his.

But he was not hers to claim.

She supposed it would be best if she relented and allowed him to give her his answer. At least they would still be able to remain friends. That was certainly her hope.

"May I have the honor of a dance, Lady Tabitha?" he asked.

The tingles of awareness returned at his use of her proper name. He rarely called her Tabitha. She rather liked the way he said it. "I would enjoy that. Thank you."

He offered his elbow, and she smiled at her friends whose interested stares suggested she would have to explain how she knew Michael when she returned after the dance.

She hadn't told anyone except Phoebe about Michael. And even then, she hadn't mentioned his name. When the league meeting was held in two weeks, she'd have to share with everyone what had happened. Until then, she could pretend he was someone more than her neighbor and childhood friend. For the moment, she could pretend he was hers.

The thought made her smile.

"What is it?" he asked.

"My friends are wondering who you are and how I know you."

"And that makes you smile?"

She glanced at him as he guided them around the guests in their path as they made their way to the dance floor. "While I don't often attend balls, rarely am I asked to dance by men like you."

"Men like me? What does that mean?" His expression suggested he was prepared to take offense.

"A handsome, eligible gentleman."

His quick, teasing smile sent her heart hammering. "Am I?"

She shook her head at his feigned innocent expression. "You know you are."

"I also know that you are an attractive, eligible lady. That makes us even."

"Not hardly." She glanced around the ballroom. "Few would consider me either." A small dowry limited her prospects as did her advancing age, mousy brown hair, lack of a figure, and plain looks. Compared to some of the ladies they passed with their blonde hair, blue eyes, and stunning gowns, she lacked in every way possible.

"I beg to differ." His frown returned. "Did everyone go blind in my absence?"

She had to laugh. With a squeeze on his arm, she sighed. "I have missed you."

Michael paused and looked down at her, his expression serious as his gaze raked her face. "I missed you as well. Times were much simpler in the past."

His quiet words were like a splash of cold water on her face. An unwelcome reminder of how complicated life had become. And a foreshadowing of his answer to her proposal.

For now, she only nodded. If she were kinder, she would come right out and tell him that he could set aside her idea. She'd say that she'd only been jesting, and of course, they couldn't do what she'd suggested.

She couldn't bring herself to say any of that. Instead, she only nodded as a heavy foreboding settled in the pit of her stomach. If only she could pretend all was well.

They reached the dance floor and took their positions.

Michael looked nervous as he glanced at the other couples nearby. Then he leaned close. "It has been some time since I've danced. Forgive me if I tread on your toes a time or two."

"I have complete faith in you," she reassured him. And she did. Not just in this, but in all matters. Though tempted to tell him so, she held back.

His eyes warmed, suggesting he appreciated her remark as he took her hand and placed his other hand on her waist in preparation for the gliding two-step of the next dance.

Tibby told herself not to place importance on the moment. It was only a dance. While she didn't dance often, it wasn't as if she never did so.

But she hadn't danced with Michael in a long time.

Would she ever again after this? The thought had her swallowing against the lump of emotion that clogged her throat. No. She wouldn't allow any sadness to gain the better of her. She would enjoy the dance and his company.

Then the music began. They moved rather awkwardly until after the first few steps.

"I told you that you'd remember," she teased, thrilled when he returned her smile. Even more thrilled when he tightened his hold on her.

"The steps are returning to me."

Tibby turned herself over to the joy of the dance, relishing in Michael's firm hold on her and the way he easily guided her across the floor. He was the perfect height, his lips even with her eyes. Those sculpted lips that so often caught her notice. His tender look when he caught her gaze sent her heart thudding.

What if...

What if by some miracle, he actually said yes? The heady thought caused her pulse to skitter, nearly making her lightheaded. She did her best to force away the question, not wanting her hopes to rise.

Yet her happiness refused to allow her to relinquish the idea that just maybe life might go her way for once. That her daring move could result in a new beginning of sorts, even if it was based on pretend.

All too soon, the dance ended. She curtsied while he bowed and then offered his arm again.

"That was lovely. Thank you," she said with sincerity.

"I enjoyed it as well. I can't think of anyone with whom I'd rather return to the dance floor than you, Tibby."

Drat that bubble of hope swelling inside her. It grew so large she could hardly breathe.

He escorted her several steps then drew to a halt, holding her hand, and looking deep into her eyes.

This was it. This was the moment. Her breath caught, the bubble enormous.

"Tibby, we can't possibly do as you suggested."

The bubble burst, leaving a sharp pain in its wake, one that caught her breath. Why hadn't she allowed him to speak with her in the garden where they could talk of this in private instead of before an entire ballroom full of acquaintances? What had she been thinking?

"It holds too great of a risk for your reputation," he continued, his brow creased with concern. "I couldn't knowingly allow you to be ruined. But know that I will put my thoughts to the task of finding another way for you to gain your freedom."

"I appreciate your concern," she managed in a level tone. "But you see, there's no reason to worry over my reputation. As a spinster, I will have little need for it. Nor do I have sisters to worry over. It's just me. And Mother." She forced a polite smile. "We'll manage. Thank you again for the dance."

With a nod, she pulled her hand from his and made her way back to where her friends still stood, wondering why she'd thought it a good idea to take such a terrible risk.

Chapter Five

Tibby waded through the following day as best she could, but her heart felt heavy, much like the ballast of a ship. Keeping busy helped to ease her disappointment but only marginally. She'd known it was unlikely Michael would say yes. Yet hope had risen until it had all but consumed her. Especially during their dance.

At least now she knew. She didn't have to wish she'd taken action and wonder what might've happened if she had.

The matter was done and that was that. She'd give a brief report at the Mayfair Literary League meeting, wish whoever decided to go next her best, and then never have to speak of her attempt again. She'd tried and could take pride in that.

Of course, she'd remain positive when she told her friends of her experience. She didn't want to discourage them from making their courageous moves.

As if sensing her daughter's minor attempt at rebellion, her mother was being especially difficult. Perhaps it was just because Tibby had attended a ball, something she hadn't done in quite some time.

If her mother had missed her and wanted her to remain home, why didn't she act kinder? It was as if she pushed Tibby until she only wanted to escape.

Instead, her mother had one complaint after another. She was too warm. Too cold. Her head hurt. Her stomach ached. No, she didn't want any tea. Why hadn't Tibby brought her tea?

It was exhausting.

Tibby didn't want Alice, the maid, to bear the brunt of her mother's displeasure, so Tibby remained in her mother's bedroom much of the day to see to her numerous requests.

But she couldn't bring herself to stay by her side the entire day. Her own mood was poor enough without constantly listening to her mother's sighs and complaints.

She stepped out of the room late that afternoon, then shut the door and leaned against it, closing her eyes briefly. The day would be easier to endure if she weren't so dispirited by Michael's refusal.

"Lady Tabitha, why don't I sit with her for a time?" Alice asked as she approached from the rear of the house.

"You have already done so much, Alice. I'm sorry she's being difficult today."

"I'm happy to help." Alice's easy smile suggested it was true. Then her brow puckered. "You don't think something is actually wrong, do you?"

"No." Her mother wasn't running a fever and her complaints varied so much that they were impossible to believe. "I think she's unhappy that I was gone last evening." Tibby hesitated to say more, not wanting to make her mother sound vindictive. "This is just her way of telling me she'd prefer I remain home."

Alice nodded, her frown easing. "I'm sure you have the right of it. I will sit with her for a time. You go have a lie-down or tend your garden. Do something relaxing."

"Are you certain?"

"Of course." Alice smiled. "Take all the time you need to clear your head, my lady." With a brief curtsy, she walked to the door and entered her mother's bedroom. "Are you feeling better, Lady Dunford?" she asked, turning to wink at Tibby before she closed the door.

Tibby sighed and turned away, realizing a break, however brief, would do her good. A breath of fresh air would be even better.

She stopped by her bedroom to retrieve her hat, shawl, and gloves, remembering she'd left her favorite gloves in Michael's greenhouse. Next, she went down to the kitchen to collect a basket. A little work in the garden would be just the thing to improve her spirits. Since it was quite late in the afternoon, it was doubtful Michael would be in the greenhouse. She wouldn't have to worry about encountering him.

The moment she stepped outside, she felt better. Once she sank onto the grass beside her garden to weed and tidy the bed, her mood lifted a bit more. Something about touching the earth and tending the plants settled her emotions as nothing else could. Each herb she touched let off a faint fragrance, adding to the calming feeling.

Staying focused on the work allowed her thoughts to settle and eased the ache in her chest. She clipped and pruned and pulled weeds to her heart's content.

"Tibby?" Michael's voice shattered that peace with only her name.

She drew a deep breath to brace herself then looked up from where she sat to see him standing alongside the wrought-iron fence. "Good afternoon, Michael. Have you been working in the greenhouse again?"

He gave a one-shouldered shrug that reminded her of his younger self. "For a time. Unfortunately, the grafting is not going any better."

She set aside her pruning shears and then rose to her feet, well aware of him watching her. The awkwardness she'd endured most of her life had her wishing she was more graceful.

Still, she walked to the fence, noting his casual brown jacket and trousers. He looked just as handsome as he had last night. But nothing compared to seeing him in only his shirt with the sleeves rolled up and his hair mussed. "I do not doubt that with practice, you will master the skill."

"I'm not certain about that," he said. "Nor do I know if I want to."

"Oh?" she asked, hoping he'd explain.

He shook his head. "That's a topic for another day. May I come over?" He gestured toward the gate their fathers had installed so the families could more easily visit each other. It hadn't been used in years.

"Of course." Hopefully, her reluctance to speak further with him wasn't obvious. She didn't want Michael to feel sorry for her but neither did she want to talk about his refusal. She only wanted to put it behind her.

He walked the few steps to the gate and unlatched it then joined her.

"I—I just wanted to see if you were all right." His gaze raked her face, his eyes more gold than green today. "I hope I didn't hurt your feelings with my refusal."

"Of course not." She shook her head, managing a smile even if she couldn't hold his gaze. "It was a silly idea anyway. I doubt it would have worked."

"You managed to go to the ball last night. Perhaps attending more functions will help your mother see that you don't intend to stay home with her all the time."

"Actually, doing so tends to have the opposite effect. Today, she has claimed no more than four different illnesses with varying aches and pains. She's made Alice's day quite difficult."

"And yours as well," he suggested.

She lifted one shoulder much as he had. "Some days are more challenging than others. Much as it is for many."

"Why do you think she does it?"

She sighed, having wondered the same. "I suppose it's a combination of issues. Loneliness. Insecurity. Grief. She was nearly overcome when Father died, and she hasn't been the same since." Tibby rubbed at some dirt on her glove as she considered the possibilities as she had many times before. "I hoped it would pass with time."

"But it hasn't."

She met his gaze at last. "If anything, it's growing worse. I should've taken more care when I first noted her unhappiness. Perhaps I should've insisted she ease back into Society. She's lost touch with most friends other than your mother."

"I'm surprised she came for a visit the other day given these details. I'm sorry. I didn't realize the situation was quite so dire."

"It is and it isn't." Tibby shook her head. "For the most part, she isn't truly ill."

"Ill in spirit."

"I suppose. I haven't found anything in particular that brings her joy. Not for long. New gowns do nothing. The prospect of visiting with old friends is much the same. Reading holds her attention only for a short time."

"She's more restless than I am."

Tibby laughed. "I hope you are faring better than my mother."

Michael didn't answer, making her wonder.

When the silence grew overlong, she added, "Her world revolved around my father. Since his death, she hasn't found a new focus."

"And that is why you thought that becoming betrothed might jolt her into rejoining life."

"Yes." That was the truth if only part of it. She really had hoped it might help her mother. Since nothing else had, the time had come for a desperate act.

However, she'd have to come up with a new one.

"Tibby." The way Michael said her name with such tenderness sent a rush of longing through her that stole her breath.

If only he said it that way out of love and affection rather than pity.

She lifted her chin, not wanting him to feel sorry for her. "Please do not concern yourself. I will think of another way to help her."

"I have no doubt you will. One that won't potentially damage your reputation." He reached out to touch her cheek, the gentle caress painful when she knew pity was behind it. "You are nowhere near becoming a spinster. You're far too wonderful to spend the rest of your days alone. The right man will come along and sweep you off your feet."

He already had. But she didn't say that. Instead, she forced a smile but eased away from his touch. She couldn't bear it. "No one knows what the future holds."

She hoped her statement sounded carefree rather than hopeless.

"I must return to Mother," Tibby said. "Enjoy your evening." She didn't meet his gaze. Instead, she stepped away to retrieve her things and hurried inside. Quickly, before she did something silly. Like tell him the real reason she'd suggested the betrothal.

DEFINITELY YES, Michael decided as the next few days crept by ever so slowly. The hopelessness in Tibby's expression had filled his days and nights, pulling at him. He simply couldn't let her down.

She needed help—had asked for *his* help—and as her friend, he wanted to be there for her.

Though he'd wracked his mind for another way to assist Lady Dunford from the doldrums that seemed to grip her, he couldn't think of any Tibby hadn't already tried.

With one last effort, he resorted to speaking to his mother about Lady Dunford to learn more about how their friendship had changed.

"I called on her numerous times in the first year after Lord Dunford passed away," she said. "She only received me a handful of times. More often than not, she refused all callers. When I did visit with her, she didn't seem to want to talk about anything other than Lord Dunford or her most recent illness. I suppose I gave up after a time."

"How difficult it must be for Tibby," he said, almost to himself.

"She has more patience than most. I confess I have been tempted to share my concern with Lady Dunford about how her behavior is affecting Tabitha. How can she not see that she's smothering the poor dear?"

Smothering. What a terrible feeling. He feared Tibby might eventually succumb to her mother's wishes for her to always remain home.

"What activities did Lady Dunford enjoy prior to her husband's death?" Michael asked. Nothing came to his mind, but he hadn't been paying attention.

"Very few. She visited with friends, did needlework, and enjoyed cards occasionally. But her life was always centered on Lord Dunford and whatever he was doing."

"What of Tibby's brother?" Michael had always liked Victor, but shouldn't he be of more help?

His mother shook her head. "He and his new wife call a few times each month but don't seem to stay very long."

Tibby's plan might force Victor to pay more attention to Lady Dunford as well. No wonder she had thought of the idea. If only she had found a man who wished to marry her.

Yet the more he thought about it, the less he liked that idea. What man would be good enough for Tibby not to mention understanding about her mother?

If he were being honest, there had been a moment at the end of their dance when the urge to kiss her had struck him. She had looked especially lovely and felt so right in his arms. Her lavender scent had tugged at him, stirring feelings that weren't platonic. He'd wanted to hold her closer and see where the moment led.

That same urge had caused him to reach out to touch her the other day in the garden. Strange, but that brief touch had only made him long for more.

He shook his head. This was Tibby. A friend in need, and he was thinking inappropriate thoughts of her.

Not so inappropriate, that voice inside reminded him.

"Michael, what did you think of Lady Sophia?" his mother asked, looking up from her needlework with a hopeful expression.

He bit back a sigh. In truth, he'd expected her to ask on the way home from the ball. She had shown great restraint by waiting this long. While he appreciated that she was trying to give him the time he'd asked for, he would've preferred she didn't ask at all.

"As I mentioned before, I'm not—" He bit off the rest of his reply, reconsidering what to say. If he decided to assist Tibby after all, he couldn't very well tell his mother he had no interest in marrying now and then suddenly tell her that he'd proposed to Tibby. "I don't think Lady Sophia is for me."

"Oh?" Her look of disappointment only made a pretend betrothal with Tibby sound more appealing.

"She is quite young. I can't help but think a more...carefree gentleman would be a better option for her." He hoped she'd let it go at that.

"In time—"

Michael held up his hand to stop her, easily guessing what she'd say—that in time, he'd become more carefree. That wasn't possible. "I truly don't think we'd suit, Mother."

Lady Sophia had been pretty with delicate features and wide blue eyes. But the few words they'd exchanged made him wonder if she had a thought in her head. Compared to Tibby, Lady Sophia seemed an empty seashell. Pretty to look at but easy to leave on the shore. He couldn't imagine courting her, let alone marrying her.

His thoughts made him realize how much he enjoyed Tibby's company. She was genuine—a good person with a heart of gold. She cared for others, could carry on an intelligent conversation with ease, and knew him so well. He remembered once again her suggestion that he find something other than botany on which to spend his time. If only he knew what that might be.

It would be no hardship to pretend to care for her. Not when he already did.

That was it. His decision was made. He would help Tibby and in turn, help himself. The relief he felt having made the choice confirmed it was the right one.

"I will leave you to your needlework," he said. "I have something I need to see to." With that, he strode from the room.

Five minutes later, he was waiting for Tibby in the Dunford drawing room. Nerves had him pacing the room. He halted in surprise. There was no reason to be nervous. This wasn't a real proposal. This was Tibby. His longtime friend.

Yet when she entered the drawing room, a look of surprise on her face, his heartbeat sped even more.

"Good afternoon, Michael." She frowned. "Is all well?"

Her question made him wonder if his unease was showing.

"Of course." He knew he sounded less than friendly, but his nervousness was annoying. Especially when he didn't understand the reason for it. After a glance over her shoulder to make certain no one would overhear, he said quietly, "I think we should proceed."

"Proceed?" She said the word as if she were unfamiliar with it.

"Yes, with your plan."

"My plan being..." Based on her confused expression, she had no idea of what he was speaking. Had she already forgotten her proposal?

Rather than answer, he lifted a brow, hoping he didn't have to be more specific. He wasn't certain he was capable of spelling it out. Not when his heart threatened to hammer its way from his chest.

"Oh." She blinked, eyes wide and lips parted as realization dawned.

Those pink lips made him want to— He cut off the thought before he could finish it. He was doing Tibby a favor. This was more for her than for him.

Why did he have to remind himself of that?

"Truly?" She studied him with disbelief.

"Truly. It seems the least I can do as your friend." There. Those words should set this conversation on the proper footing.

It took only half a moment for him to realize he'd said the wrong thing.

"The least." She glanced away. "I certainly wouldn't want to inconvenience you."

"No." He stepped forward. "That isn't what I meant."

"It isn't?" Her raised brow suggested he needed to say more.

But what? "It is not an inconvenience." He searched his mind for what more he could say. "Nothing of the sort. It is for my benefit as well."

She continued to watch him, her expression making it clear she was less than convinced of his sincerity.

"It would be my privilege," he tried again. "And it will help me." He gestured toward his home. "Mother continually speaks of me finding a wife and has already introduced me to one candidate. That's the last thing I want." He pressed a hand to his brow, hoping he was making himself clear. His thoughts were so muddled he wasn't sure.

"Are you certain about this?" she asked, her eyes still wide as if she couldn't quite believe he'd changed his mind. "I thought we'd both agreed it wasn't a good idea after all."

"I'm positive." He nodded despite the doubt swirling through his mind. "It's the solution to both of our problems."

She stared at him for a long moment. Until his breath started to hitch in his chest. Why was she hesitating? He wanted—needed—her to agree, not that he could explain the reason behind it. Not when his thoughts were caught by those wide brown eyes the color of dark chocolate, long black lashes, and those rosy, full lips perfect for kissing.

Kissing? He huffed out a breath. What was wrong with him?

"Very well. We shall proceed." She reached out her hand for him to take. "Thank you."

A handshake? To confirm a betrothal? Yet he found himself taking her hand and shaking it all the same. This was growing stranger by the moment.

"*For Better or Worse*," she said.

"Excuse me?"

Her mouth gaped, and she quickly shook her head. "Never mind. Yes. We are in agreement."

"You mean, we are betrothed." His chest tightened even more at the thought. Why didn't it feel like pretend?

Chapter Six

Tibby released Michael's hand, unable to believe the sudden turn of events. Or rather, of her life.

Betrothed.

Thinking about it was one thing. Experiencing it was quite another.

She released a quiet breath. A *pretend* betrothal. That was the important part to remember. Their arrangement was not real. It was up to her to make Michael see that they would suit. That he cared for her more than he realized and as more than a friend. Much more.

The task sounded impossible. Yet she'd gotten this far. That alone was proof miracles were possible.

She couldn't believe she'd mentioned the *For Better or Worse* agenda. Thank goodness Michael hadn't pressed her for an explanation of why she'd said that or what it meant.

"Are you certain this...arrangement will serve the purpose you want?" he asked quietly.

No, she nearly blurted. Then she gathered her thoughts, wondering how best to answer.

"Given how...unhappy your mother has been since you attended the ball," Michael continued, "don't you think she will feel even worse once we share our news?"

"She might." Tibby nodded. "In fact, I'm certain she will. But my hope is that her dismay will be temporary. Once she's adjusted to our...betrothal, I intend to use it as a reason to insist she attend a few functions as well as spend time with friends."

"How so?" He frowned.

"There are social gatherings and outings that are expected before a lady marries, from additional visits to the modiste for new gowns to dinners and all the rest." She waved a hand to dismiss the details. She didn't know for certain what was involved, having never been betrothed. For all she knew, none of what she'd said was true.

Her only friend that had experienced a betrothal was Phoebe, and hers was anything but ordinary.

"When shall we tell our families?" she asked.

Rather than immediately answering, Michael stared into the distance as if considering the possibilities. "Perhaps we should ease into this before we share the news."

"Ease into it?" She wasn't quite sure to what he was referring.

"In order for it to be believable, at least for our immediate family, we should show more of an interest in each other."

"Of course." Tibby nodded, though she couldn't think what that might entail given that they were already friends and spoke often.

"I will begin formally calling on you." His gaze swung to hold hers. "We'll have to hint at deepening feelings between us."

It was all Tibby could do not to press a hand to her chest to calm her racing heart. She needed to hide how overwhelmed she was by this. And nervous. It was supposed to be pretend.

"We already know each other well, so that shouldn't be overly difficult."

"True. Perhaps a week or two of that will show them that our regard for one another has deepened."

She nodded. "Very well."

"We'll need to make sure we do so while with them as well as when we're alone in case they're watching. Does that sound reasonable?"

"Yes." Tibby was proud her voice didn't squeak when she answered. She couldn't quite wrap her mind around what they might do or say to make certain their families were prepared for what was coming.

Even she wasn't prepared for it.

Michael smiled and moved closer to take her hand. "We should make use of every possible moment."

She stared at their linked hands, her knees growing weak at the contact. How was she going to manage anything more than a small touch without revealing her true feelings?

"It might take practice," Michael suggested.

"Practice. Yes." That was something to which Tibby could readily agree. Though she worried that doing so might toss her in over her head if she wasn't already.

"We should make it clear we want to be together in every way."

"Every way," she repeated. Was he speaking of general shows of affection, like a brief touch, or something more substantial, like kissing? How she wished she was brave enough to ask if only to better prepare herself.

He trailed a finger along her cheek, sending a sizzle of awareness down her spine. It was all she could do not to shiver in response. "This should be fun." Then he smiled. But it wasn't the teasing one she was used to. It held something else.

Fun? To what precisely did he refer? Them showing affection or them fooling their families? Guilt rushed in, smothering the sizzle.

She truly was in over her head.

"Why don't you come by the greenhouse in the morning so we can discuss it further? That will give both of us some time to think about it. Then perhaps I should call on you tomorrow afternoon."

"Very well."

He released her hand and stepped back, not seeming the least affected by the moment. "If all goes well, we might be able to tell them of our betrothal within a few days. We will see how convincing we can be."

Tibby stared at him, reminding herself that this was what she'd wanted for numerous reasons. Yet why did she feel like she wasn't going to emerge from this unscathed? She couldn't help but think of that wise saying about being careful what you wished for, lest it comes true.

THE NEXT MORNING, MICHAEL was back in the greenhouse to check on the progress of his grafting. It was too soon to tell whether his attempts would be successful, but he had to do something to keep his thoughts occupied and away from Tibby. At least for a time.

He considered the clay pots filled with stems lined up neatly in a row. Surely doing more would increase the chances of success.

He'd expected to feel relief after his conversation with Tibby. He had stepped forward to help a friend and doing so would benefit him as well. But those few moments of holding her hand and speaking of what they needed to do to convince their relatives that their feelings were genuine had been unsettling.

He frowned as he retrieved three empty pots from a nearby shelf. That wasn't the right word. Enlightening? Perhaps.

At any rate, those moments had made him reconsider just what he felt for Tibby. Friendship, for certain. But damn if there wasn't something more between them.

He needed to take care. The last thing he wanted to do was jeopardize their friendship. He was supposed to be helping Tibby, not hurting her. She trusted him to aid her. He didn't want to break that trust.

The door to the greenhouse opened, and he couldn't deny the anticipation that shot through him. To his disappointment, his mother stepped inside.

"Good morning, Michael," she said with a bright smile. "I was going to the garden and thought I'd check to see how your experiments are coming along."

"They are holding up thus far." He gestured toward the row of stems in pots. "Time will tell. I thought I would try a few more in case those aren't successful."

"How industrious of you." She leaned close to look at the stems. "They look quite healthy."

"So did the last batch just before they died."

Before she could respond, the door opened again.

And once again, Michael's heartbeat sped.

"Good morning." Tibby's eyes went wide at the sight of his mother at his side, and she halted. "I'm sorry. I didn't mean to interrupt."

"How lovely to see you, Tabitha," his mother greeted her. "Did you come to see how Michael's roses are coming along?"

"Yes." Tibby nodded enthusiastically. Perhaps too much so, for his mother's eyes narrowed slightly as if she were puzzled by her response. "How do they look?"

"It's too early to say," Michael said as he glanced at them again. "I thought I'd do a few more in case these fail."

"Very wise of you," Tibby said, still standing by the door, clearly uncertain if she should stay.

Michael stepped back, out of his mother's line of vision, and waved for her to come forward.

Tibby's cheeks turned a delightful shade of pink as she walked closer. "Will these be a different type or are you repeating your latest efforts?"

Michael's mother eased back to make room for Tibby to view the pots. The narrow aisle meant they were standing close together.

"The same, I think."

Tibby nodded. "Did you give any further thought to my suggestion about other activities?"

Michael was surprised she'd mention the idea in front of his mother. "I have, though nothing has come to mind."

"What other activities?" his mother asked.

"I thought another hobby might prove more satisfying," Tibby said.

"Such as what?" Michael asked. While he would agree that he didn't have a burning desire for botany, it was interesting and held his attention. He enjoyed reading about it but couldn't imagine spending more than an hour or two working on it.

Tibby's lips twisted as if she were uncertain, her gaze holding on the pots and then glancing at both of them before her gaze shifted to him. "I think you should write a novel."

Michael hid his disappointment. He thought Tibby knew him better than to recommend something so outlandish.

"A novel?" His mother studied him, clearly curious about what he thought of the idea. "How interesting." She turned to Tibby. "You mean about his experiences in the military?"

"No, although that is certainly an option." Tibby's eyes glittered with excitement as they held on his, making him think she'd given the topic serious consideration. "A mystery. A clever plot filled with twists and turns and the darker side of life. Your letters always painted a picture of the places you'd seen and the people around you. They were so vivid that I felt as if I were with you."

"That's true," his mother agreed. "I came to know some of the men who served with you through your descriptions."

"Letters are different. I don't know anything about writing a book." Yet the more he thought about it, the more intriguing it was. Much more than he would've guessed. Was that due to Tibby thinking he was capable of it?

"You've always liked to read," Tibby said. "That's one of the activities we've both enjoyed." Again, her cheeks pinkened. She glanced at his mother from under her lashes as if worried about what she might be thinking before looking again at him. "You're in need of a challenge. Writing would certainly be one."

"I wouldn't know how to begin." But the more he considered the idea, the more he thought he might want to try.

"I think it's an excellent idea." His mother's genuine enthusiasm was sweet. She looked between them, making Michael wonder if their plan was already working. "I will leave the two of you to discuss it further." She walked toward the door only to turn back. "I look forward to hearing what you decide."

Then she was gone, leaving Michael and Tibby alone.

Michael studied Tibby. Had she only made the suggestion that he write a mystery as part of their plan to show their families that their relationship was starting to change? The idea was disappointing. Exactly why, he couldn't say.

"Were you serious?" he found himself asking.

"Yes. Very much." Again, her eyes shone with excitement. "You see situations differently than most. And you are so observant, noting details that few others see. You're well read, clever, creative, and a quick learner. I think you would make an exceptional author."

Her belief in him was more than heartwarming. It was inspiring. If she asked him to swim across the ocean and listed the reasons she thought he could, he'd certainly try.

"What do you think?" she asked. "Will you consider the idea?" She glanced at the row of pots. "It wouldn't mean you have to abandon botany."

"You think I'm capable of doing both?" He smiled, rewarded when she returned it.

"I do. That and so much more."

He moved closer, drawn like a puppet on a string. "Tibby."

"Yes?"

"You are amazing."

Doubt flickered in her eyes. "I'm merely logical."

"The idea of me writing a novel is not logical. But it is intriguing. Surprisingly so." He reached for her hand, the urge to hug her nearly overwhelming. The urge to kiss her was even more so. He settled for pressing a kiss on her cheek, noting how she stiffened.

The chaste kiss was unsatisfying. Did she feel the same? Hadn't he said they needed to become accustomed to showing affection? This was the perfect chance to test them both. When they were alone, and their reaction wouldn't be observed.

He eased close, his focus on her lips. She remained still as if uncertain of what he intended. But her breath was coming quickly. So was his.

Desire swirled through him, and he leaned even closer. Nothing about the moment felt wrong. Did that mean it was right?

Then his thoughts fell away, and he kissed her. Her lips were stiff with the same surprise that held the rest of her. Within seconds, she softened, then hesitantly kissed him in return.

The urge to deepen it nearly took over, but he held back, not wanting to move too quickly. He didn't think either of them was prepared for that. But he wouldn't deny how strong the urge was to do so. Surprisingly strong. The need racing through him had nothing to do with platonic friendship.

He pulled back to look into her brown eyes. A mix of surprise and passion was evident in their warm depths. Then she bit her lip and the small gesture shot straight through him.

Definitely not mere friendship. Then what? He was suddenly eager to find out.

Chapter Seven

Lady Dunford stared at Michael like he was an oddity at a museum. Like she couldn't understand what he was doing in her drawing room.

He was relieved to know that Tibby wanted him there or he might've found a polite way to excuse himself and depart as quickly as his feet could carry him.

The realization of how a suitor might be treated by the lady of the house—if one had ever called—stirred his sympathies for Tibby even more.

"How kind of you to call," Tibby said in the awkward silence that filled the room after the butler had announced him.

Michael caught the pointed look Tibby sent her mother.

"Yes," Lady Dunford said. "So kind." She looked past his shoulder. "Your mother and grandmother aren't joining us?"

"Not this time." Hopefully, she'd hear the implied message that there would be more calls in the near future.

"Please have a seat." Tibby gestured toward a blue wingback chair as she and her mother settled on the matching settee.

"Thank you." He gave an easy smile and took a seat, casting a quick look about the room. He hadn't paid the décor any attention on his previous visit.

Much like his home, little had changed since his numerous visits well over a decade ago. But here, the furnishings had faded and looked slightly worn, causing him to wonder if there weren't extra funds for updates.

Or perhaps it was a reflection of Lady Dunford's frequent illnesses. Her attention was focused on how she felt rather than appearances. Since they had few visitors, the shabbiness of the decor could be easily pushed aside.

His gaze shifted to Tibby. No wonder she'd formed a plan to jolt her mother out of this decline and give both herself and Lady Dunford a future, or at least the chance of one.

"How are you finding life in London now that you've had a chance to settle in?" Lady Dunford asked.

Michael studied her for a moment as he considered how to answer. Much like the furnishings, her gown had seen better days. The muslin's once bright stripes were now dull. But it was her eyes that held his attention. They had a flat look to them that suggested she found little in life that brought her joy.

The loss of her husband had obviously devastated her. His own mother had been distraught, too, but had done her best to pick up the pieces of her life and take enjoyment in her children and the rest of the family, as well as her friends.

Michael had never considered that his mother might remarry. It was an odd thought and made him uncomfortable. But if she found someone to make her happy, he certainly wouldn't stand in her way.

How fortunate that Tibby had chosen to act now lest it be too late for Lady Dunford to adjust to a life not completely spent in her bedroom.

"It was difficult at first, but I have found some activities that bring me joy." Remembering the purpose of his visit, he looked again at Tibby and smiled. "My friendship with Lady Tabitha is one of those."

Tibby's eyes darkened even as a blush rose in her cheeks. For some reason, her response made him think of their kiss. Kisses and Tibby shouldn't go together yet they did. So much so that he looked forward to sharing another.

"Oh?" Lady Dunford's brow puckered as if she were confused as she glanced between them. "I suppose I had forgotten how much time the two of you spent together when you were children. I'm sure you have other friends as well."

"A few." He allowed his gaze to linger on Tibby, hoping her mother noticed.

"Will you share some of your adventures with us?" Lady Dunford asked, seeming determined to steer the conversation away from her daughter.

He hesitated, trying to sift through a memorable moment that hadn't involved bloodshed. "Military life is often difficult, of course. But I suppose seeing other countries was one of the benefits. The mountains in New Zealand are spectacular."

Tibby lifted a brow, her interest clearly piqued. That was enough to have him describe some of what he'd seen, including descriptions of the craggy, snow-capped peaks, and the interesting animals that called the country home.

"And what of Australia?" Tibby asked. "Did you see a kangaroo?"

Even her mother listened with interest as he shared a story of an encounter with the unusual creature and the first time he'd caught sight of a koala bear.

"I saw one at the zoo when I was younger." Tibby glanced at her mother. "Do you remember? We went with Father and Victor."

Lady Dunford stared out the window for so long that he thought she wouldn't answer. Finally, she nodded. "That was an enjoyable day."

Tibby's lips twisted as she watched her mother.

"How is Victor?" Michael asked, thinking it best to change the subject. "I have yet to see him since my return."

"He is well," Tibby said. "I'm sure you'll meet his wife, Elizabeth, soon. We enjoy her company very much."

"They don't visit often," Lady Dunford said, still staring out the window.

"Perhaps not as often as we'd like." The look Tibby cast her mother suggested the conversation was well worn, much like the furniture. "But we've been invited numerous times to their home and have rarely gone."

"They should come here instead. He knows I don't care to venture out."

Michael shifted in his seat, wishing he could think of another topic that might please Lady Dunford.

"We shall invite them for tea again," Tibby suggested. "Perhaps Michael could join us so you could meet Victor's wife."

"I would like that," he said warmly.

They visited for a little while longer before he moved to the edge of his chair. "I should be going."

Tibby stood when he did. "I will see you out," she offered.

"But he just lives next door," her mother protested.

Michael had to wonder if she was already realizing their plan.

"He's a dear friend who called," Tibby said with a lift of her chin. "I will see him to the door."

Michael was pleased she didn't submit to all of her mother's wishes. Though their disagreements were minor, they had to wear on Tibby when she endured them each and every day. Michael's admiration for her increased another notch.

He followed her out of the drawing room and down the stairs, pausing in the entrance hall. If her butler hadn't been standing nearby, he might've reached for her hand.

The realization caught him by surprise. He needed to remember the pretend component of this relationship.

"Thank you for calling," she said.

"The pleasure was mine. I look forward to doing so again." With a nod, he departed. Only when he had nearly returned to his house did he realize they hadn't decided on their next step.

He paused to look back at Tibby's house, debating on whether to speak with her now, only to see her mother watching him from the drawing room window. Their eyes met, then she gave a small shake of her head and turned away.

Hmm. He had to think that Lady Dunford wasn't pleased with the new development in her daughter's life. That only made him more determined to see their plan through so Tibby could have some hope for the future despite her mother's lack of interest in one.

THE NEXT MORNING, TIBBY practically danced in her bedroom as she prepared for the day. She managed to curb her good spirits when Alice arrived to help her dress.

"Aren't you in a fine mood this morning, Lady Tabitha," Alice remarked as she laced her corset.

"I am." How could she not be when the plan was going so well?

Her mother had remarked on the oddness of Michael's visit when Tibby had returned to the drawing room after she'd seen him to the door. "I have no idea why he thought he needed to call on us."

Tibby had felt the weight of her regard. This was her chance to make what was coming clear. She'd seized it with both hands. "We have had a few conversations since his return," she began. "I confess that my feelings for him are growing."

"A friendship is just that. A friendship. Don't make it more than it is." Her mother had sniffed.

"I think it might indeed be more." Rather than remain to argue, Tibby had quickly excused herself and left Alice to sit with her mother for a time.

Michael had sent a message, asking her to come by the greenhouse in the morning if possible so they could decide what their next steps would be. Having the meeting to look forward to made it easier to endure the dour looks her mother sent her way.

Last evening, dinner had been a stilted affair, her mother's poor mood obvious. Though Tibby felt guilty to be the cause of it, she held back from apologizing—or worse, telling her the truth.

This was for her mother's own good. She wasn't happy. Surely trying new activities to bring her out of the house would aid her. Tibby need only be patient and continually encourage her.

Tibby had read to her before bed as usual. But by the time she'd sought her own bed, she was exhausted from striving for a balance between countering her mother's negative remarks and ignoring them.

The thought of seeing Michael at the greenhouse again made it easier to forget—and forgive—her mother's behavior.

"Is Lady Dunford still sleeping?" Tibby asked.

"Yes. She might have a bit of a lie-in this morning as it took her some time to fall asleep last night."

Alice or one of the other maids stayed with her mother until she slept. She didn't like to be alone at that time of the evening. Tibby occasionally did as well but given that she spent nearly all day every day with her, the maids insisted they were happy to sit with her.

"I'm sorry to hear that," Tibby said, guilt dimming her happiness.

Michael's visit had obviously upset her mother even more than Tibby had realized. Deep inside, she'd hoped her mother might be excited for her. Thrilled that her daughter might have found someone.

How silly.

"Please let me know when she wakes."

"Of course, my lady."

After Tibby went downstairs for a light breakfast, she checked the time. The hour was still early, but she wanted—needed—to see Michael, if only for a few minutes.

She retrieved her shawl then informed the butler where she was going in case any problem arose. After stepping out of the garden door, she slipped through the gate and into the Trafford Garden, her heart lifting at the sight of the greenhouse.

As she neared it, Michael came out. Her entire body tightened at the sight of his handsome visage.

"Tibby." His broad smile caught her by surprise, making her breathless. "How good to see you."

"Good morning."

He walked forward and took both her hands in his.

Oh my. The way he looked into her eyes and held her hands made her heart hammer with delight. She had to find a way to make him a permanent part of her future rather than just temporary.

"I'm so pleased you came by," he said.

She thought that was what they'd agreed on, but she still appreciated his warm greeting.

He glanced toward the second story of his house, making her wonder why. But how could she be bothered with the question when he then stared into her eyes as if he was happy to see her?

Her heart fluttered at the thought.

"How was your evening?" He tucked her hand under his arm and led her along one of the garden paths with slow steps.

"Rather uneventful." She smiled up at him, hesitating to tell him about her mother. "And yours?"

"Much the same." He paused and turned to face her, reaching for her hand again. "How is Lady Dunford today?"

"Still resting." She shook her head. "She wasn't especially happy after your visit yesterday, but I did my best to ignore her remarks."

"I know it must be a challenge. I certainly admire the way you care for her. It seems as if your brother doesn't help as much as he should."

"He used to come more frequently, but mother made it a habit to list her complaints when he did. If I were him, I probably wouldn't visit often either. I've tried to explain that she should talk about other things to no avail."

Again, he glanced at his house as if looking for something.

"Is all well?" she asked, wondering at his odd behavior.

"Quite. Upon my return home yesterday, I advised Mother and Grandmother that I had called on you. Hopefully, they are starting to understand what that means." He reached out and cupped her cheek, the tender gesture squeezing her heart.

How was she supposed to remember this was pretend when he made such sweet gestures?

"How did they take the news?" she asked.

"Grandmother seemed puzzled, but Mother smiled and told me that I was a good friend to you."

"That wasn't exactly what we were hoping for. I suppose it might take time for them to see our intentions." Dismay swept over Tibby. Of course, his family couldn't imagine more between them when she was still plain Tibby who hadn't caught the attention of a suitor in years.

"Perhaps we can find a way around that." He leaned close then closer still.

Was he truly going to kiss her here? Alarm speared through her at the thought. But not enough to pull back. Desire took over, dismissing the alarm.

The kiss shocked her to her toes even though she knew it was coming. His lips fit hers perfectly. His experience was clear. She didn't think she'd ever become accustomed to his kisses.

When her legs weakened, she found herself leaning into him.

He reached for her waist, his hands holding her firmly. Still feeling unsteady, she reached up to place her hands on his chest. Somehow, the physical touch did little to settle her reeling thoughts.

Just when she hoped he might deepen the kiss, he eased back and looked into her eyes once again.

Oh. My. She could only blink up at him, stunned by the feelings coursing through her.

"That should help," he murmured.

"Help what?" she managed, sounding as if she had a frog in her throat.

"Help to convince my mother, who is watching us from her sitting room window."

His explanation sank in slowly. Her heart sank as well. Of course, he hadn't been that pleased to see her. This had all been a ploy to convince his mother that they were interested in each other.

She told herself to be happy that he was taking the plan so seriously. If his mother had witnessed their kiss, she wouldn't be surprised when they announced their betrothal.

But part of her longed for him to have been happy to see her. To have wanted to kiss her of his own accord.

Had he even enjoyed it? She thought he had. Hoped he had. Then again, she had no experience with such things. Still, she couldn't believe all kisses were like that one.

"I won't look to see if she's still watching," he said. "But just in case, shall we walk for a time?"

"Certainly." She forced a smile. Somehow, she had to remember to keep her wits about her when she was with Michael. And especially when they kissed.

That didn't mean she couldn't store away these moments in her memory to pull out if her plan didn't work and she was alone in the coming years. If only the kisses they'd shared didn't mean so much to her. She needed to take care, remaining hopeful but not falling head over heels for this man.

"Shall we discuss our next step?" she asked, proud of herself for sounding calm. She could do this, couldn't she?

Chapter Eight

Michael entered Tibby's drawing room three days later, worry weighing heavily on his shoulders. She had arranged for Victor and his wife to come for tea, and he had been invited as well. The plan was for Michael to have a moment to speak alone with Victor Malton, the Earl of Dunford, to ask for her hand in marriage.

In the days since he'd kissed her in the garden, they'd managed several occasions together to show their families how close they were becoming.

He'd gone so far as to tell his mother how much he cared for Tibby. Yet he couldn't deny the guilt that warred with the need to help Tibby—and himself—with their plan. At times, he wondered if he should've just told his mother what they were doing.

However, he had no doubt that she would disapprove. Nor would it solve his own problem of wanting to be free from her constant remarks about finding a wife.

The reasons for her disapproval would be valid, which didn't sit well with him either. She would have the same worry that he did—what would happen to Tibby after they broke off the betrothal?

It was too late to act on his second thoughts. He and Tibby had started down this path, and he was committed to seeing it through to the conclusion.

He didn't understand why the betrothal felt so real at times. As if he and Tibby would get along well if all this were actually happening.

What had rattled him was kissing her. Enjoying it was one thing. As he'd previously acknowledged, he was a man with normal wants and needs. But the extent to which he looked forward to more of those moments shocked him.

Desire was only part of his growing admiration for Tibby. Her care and regard for her mother despite the difficulty of the situation were amazing. Then there was the way she made him feel. He could be himself without the need to wear a mask, pretending to be or feel something he wasn't. Especially not when only the two of them were together.

Even now, his gaze met hers and his world settled. He would hazard a guess that he wasn't the only one nervous based on how tightly she clasped her hands before her as she stood to greet him.

Tibby's mother gave him a polite, if cool, smile but remained seated.

"Good to see you again, Shaw." Dunford stood to shake his hand.

"You as well. It's been a long time."

Lord Dunford looked much as Michael remembered with brown hair a shade darker than Tibby's. It was clipped short and combed to one side. Long sideburns narrowed his face, but he'd appeared to have gained a stone or two in the last decade.

"May I introduce my wife, Lady Elizabeth?"

Michael bowed. "It's a pleasure, my lady. Lady Tabitha speaks highly of you."

"How kind of her." Tibby's sister-in-law was a rather plain woman with brown hair, a plump figure, and a kind face. She seemed distracted, continually glancing at her mother-in-law as if concerned about what the older woman might say.

"Tibby tells me you've sold your commission." Dunford gestured for Michael to sit then he and his wife did so as well.

"Yes. The time had come to return home."

"I hope the adjustment has gone smoothly."

Michael's gaze sought Tibby's without him thinking twice. "It was rather difficult at first but has quickly improved."

Tibby smiled in response.

Michael made certain to hold her gaze for a long moment. If Dunford were paying attention, he would soon notice more was going on between them than simple friendship.

Tibby poured tea once it arrived. He was pleasantly surprised when she remembered he preferred his tea black and placed his favorite sandwiches and biscuits on his plate before handing it to him. Her thoughtfulness never failed to touch him.

Lady Dunford said little as they enjoyed the tea, her attention holding on her son while nibbling on one of the sandwiches and sipping her tea.

Michael wondered at her thoughts. From what Tibby had said at different times over the last few days, Lady Dunford was continuing to make life difficult with her frequent complaints and supposed illnesses with ever-changing symptoms.

The conversation moved from Dunford speaking about a few issues before the House of Lords to upcoming social functions.

"We don't attend many events, but I am looking forward to the Barrington Ball," his wife said with a smile at her husband. "It should be an entertaining evening."

"That particular ball was always a pleasure, but I don't think I'll feel well enough to attend this year." Lady Dunford heaved a beleaguered sigh.

"Hmm." Dunford's lips twisted as he regarded his mother. "It seems you haven't felt well enough to go the last several years."

Tibby kept her gaze fixed on her plate. Surely, she was ready for her brother to deal with their mother for a change.

"My constitution isn't what it used to be." Lady Dunford's chin lifted, a hint of stubbornness gleaming in her eyes.

"Doing something you used to enjoy might help to improve it," her daughter-in-law said with a tight smile. "Perhaps you could attend the ball even if just for a brief time."

"Yes, Mother." Tibby gave an encouraging nod to her sister-in-law. "Elizabeth may be right. You haven't seen your friends for an age. I'm sure they'd be delighted to visit with you. That would lift your spirits."

Michael waited to see how Lady Dunford would respond, watching Tibby's hopeful expression. Would this be the moment Tibby had hoped for? That her mother would return to her former life and no longer depend on her daughter so heavily?

While that would be wonderful for Tibby and her family, especially Lady Dunford, he suddenly realized how terrible it would be for him. He liked helping Tibby. He liked being needed. Most of all, he liked Tibby and this new relationship they were forming.

What he didn't like was the thought of ending their association before it had even begun. Not yet. Not until—

He cut off the thought, uncertain where it might lead.

"I will see how I feel the day of the ball." Lady Dunford shook her head. "It seems doubtful that I would have the energy to go even for a short time."

"We shall hope for the best," Lady Elizabeth said with a resigned look at both her husband and Tibby.

The look suggested the three had dealt with similar conversations before without success.

Michael released the breath he hadn't realized he'd been holding. How dreadful of him not to want Lady Dunford to make a miraculous recovery. Not yet anyway.

After everyone had finished their tea, Michael cleared his throat. "I wonder if I might speak with you in private for a moment, Dunford."

"Of course." Tibby's brother was clearly curious and gestured for Michael to follow him out the door.

"I see your brother and his wife on occasion," Dunford said as he led the way down the stairs to the reception room near the front hall. "I'm sure he and the rest of your family are pleased you have returned."

"It is good to be home and enjoy a few more creature comforts than what military life offers." Michael drew a quick breath, hoping to settle the hint of nerves dancing in his stomach. Those nerves surprised him when none of this was real.

Dunford closed the door behind them and turned to face Michael. "What can I help you with?"

"I would like to ask for your blessing to marry Lady Tabitha."

Dunford stilled, eyes wide with surprise. Then a broad smile came over his expression, and he stepped forward to shake Michael's hand with enthusiasm. "Yes, of course. That is fine news. Fine news, indeed. Tibby is in agreement, I assume?"

"Yes, we've discussed it." Michael hesitated. "Of course, she's worried about how your mother will take the news."

"As am I. However, I was even more worried about Tibby's future. I didn't want her to be forced to take care of our mother for the rest of her years."

"I'm sorry Lady Dunford seems so unhappy." Michael didn't bother to use the term 'ill' when that didn't seem to be the case.

"We have tried numerous ways to convince her to step back into life. But the situation seems to worsen rather than improve with each year that passes. It's as if she's determined to be displeased with her lot." Dunford waved a hand in dismissal. "That discussion is for another time. We shall focus on the good news today. Congratulations."

"Thank you." However, Dunford's happiness dimmed Michael's when guilt returned in full force. He didn't like the idea of fooling their families even if it hadn't seemed like a problem when they'd made this plan.

"Why don't you stop by in the coming weeks so we can discuss the settlement?" the earl asked as he clapped a hand on Michael's shoulder.

"I look forward to it."

"Perhaps you'd allow me a few minutes with my family to share the news."

"Of course."

"I'll send Tibby down momentarily." Dunford walked to the door, glancing back at Michael with another smile.

Michael managed to return it but groaned the moment the earl stepped out of sight. Lying was more difficult than he'd anticipated.

"WHAT WAS THAT ALL ABOUT?" Tibby's mother asked when Victor returned to the drawing room.

Tibby bolted to her feet, her focus holding on her brother.

His grin as he walked directly to her suggested he was more than pleased with what Michael had asked him. His warm embrace confirmed it.

The moment would have been wonderful if Tibby's conscience hadn't been getting the better of her. Still, she returned her brother's hug and his smile.

"We have much to celebrate," Victor said as he went to sit beside Elizabeth.

"Oh?" Tibby's mother frowned.

Tibby wanted to stomp her foot in protest. How could her mother pretend she didn't know when Tibby and Michael had made it clear where their relationship was moving during the past few days?

Tibby held her silence, relieved Victor was there to help manage their mother's reaction. Tibby knew she'd pay for the news over the coming days and weeks. However, she hoped it would make her mother realize she needed to reach for happiness unless she wanted to spend the years ahead alone.

Tibby continued to hope the pretend betrothal was the key to her own happy future as well. She held tight to the thought and her smile, pushing aside her remorse for deceiving those she loved.

"Captain Shaw has asked for our Tibby's hand in marriage," Victor announced.

Her mother's expression didn't change. Not one bit.

"How wonderful." Elizabeth rose to hug Tibby. "I'm overjoyed for you, dear sister."

"Thank you." Tibby returned her embrace. She'd always liked Elizabeth. If not for her mother's behavior, she thought the two of them would be closer. Perhaps that might still happen.

Elizabeth turned to look at her husband then back at Tibby with a grin. "I could tell from the way Captain Shaw watched you that he was smitten."

Tibby's heart pinched. If only that were true, and Michael hadn't been acting.

"Do tell," Elizabeth said with a teasing glint in her eyes. "Is it a love match?"

Tibby's cheeks heated. "Of a sort." What else could she say? Besides, it might be true. Time would tell. She certainly cared for him. That made it half-true.

"You've known each other since you were children and have been friends this whole time." Her mother jerked to her feet, hands clenched at her sides. "It makes no sense that you've suddenly become something more."

"Feelings change," Tibby managed, more hurt than she would've guessed possible.

"Yes, they do," Elizabeth agreed with a nod. "After he was gone for so long, that's only natural."

Again, Tibby was grateful Victor and Elizabeth were there so that she didn't have to bear the brunt of her mother's reaction on her own. If only they were staying longer.

Her mother folded her arms over her chest. "I don't like it."

"Mother." Victor studied her with a stern expression. "You only say that because you want to keep Tibby at your side."

"That's not true." The sharp edge to her mother's tone caused Tibby to stiffen, her stomach tightening.

She hated disagreements, especially when they involved her. But there was no avoiding this one. She'd known that from the start.

"Then why aren't you pleased?" Victor asked, his frustration clear. "You like Michael. Father liked him as well. So do I."

"Everyone is to be happy except me." Her mother's chest heaved with her upset.

"No one wants you to be upset." Tibby drew close, hoping to reach her. "We want nothing more than to see you enjoy yourself and start living again."

"How can I when I'll be left alone?"

Tibby's emotions spun at the statement. That was her fear as well. Michael had departed for the army, her father had died, then her brother had married Elizabeth. And she was left here with her mother. Not that she didn't love her, but there had to be more to life.

Would she be able to bear it if she had to call off the betrothal with Michael?

"That's your choice, Mother," Victor insisted. "You have to understand how difficult it is for us to visit often when all you speak about is how unwell you feel."

Tibby hid a grimace. She wished he hadn't brought that up when doing so would only send their mother into a downward spiral of yet another illness.

"You would prefer I hold back the truth when you ask how I am?"

"Nothing of the sort," Elizabeth said. "However, it would be nice if the conversation moved on to other topics as well."

"I cannot believe this." Her mother waved a trembling hand in the air, her entire body shaking. "How can I feel anything but attacked by your remarks?"

"It is not intended that way, Mother." Tibby held her gaze. "We love you and want to see you happy."

"Forgive me if I find that impossible to believe." She turned on her heel and hurried out of the room.

Tibby closed her eyes and sighed. She'd feared telling her mother would go poorly but part of her had hoped otherwise.

"I'm sorry, Tibby," Victor said. "This should be a celebratory occasion."

"Don't let her spoil it for you." Elizabeth squeezed Tibby's hand. "She's just worried that you'll leave her."

"Now she knows Tibby will," Victor countered.

The urge to tell them the truth had Tibby pressing her lips tight. She'd come this far. She couldn't give in now. This was for her mother's sake as much as her own.

"At any rate, we are delighted for you." Elizabeth looked over her shoulder at Victor, and he moved closer to join them.

"Yes, we are." His grin eased the vise around Tibby's chest. "Very pleased. Shaw is a good man."

"He is." Tibby breathed a little easier. "Such a good man." That she knew for a fact.

Now that they'd reached this point, it was up to her to show him that she was perfect for him. If only she knew how.

"He's waiting in the reception room if you'd like a moment together," her brother said.

"Oh." Tibby's heart leapt, her upset lessening. "I would like that very much. Thank you." She hugged both Victor and Elizabeth. "I won't be long."

"Take your time," Elizabeth called with a laugh.

This is just pretend. This is just pretend.

She repeated the phrase under her breath all the way down the stairs. That didn't keep joy from bubbling up inside her.

She paused in the open doorway of the reception room and smiled. The sight of Michael standing there waiting for her made her heart take flight. "Victor is very pleased."

"I'm glad to hear it," he said, returning her smile.

Tibby continued forward to stand before him. "Of course, Mother isn't happy."

Michael grimaced. "I was afraid of that. I suppose it was to be expected."

"I wish she could find joy in something."

"I'm sure your brother and his wife feel the same way. Let us hope that our betrothal will set her on the right path."

"I can't thank you enough for helping me." She wanted him to understand how much it meant to her. To think he thought enough of her, if only as a friend, to do this was heartwarming. She had to hope it would lead to more.

"It's aiding me as well," he said. "Shall we determine our next steps?"

"Do you have something in mind?"

"I intend to share our betrothal with my family upon my return home."

She nodded, wondering how Lady Trafford would take the news, along with his grandmother. Would they be happy or disappointed?

Once again, a mantle of guilt settled over her. She detested that they were deceiving their families even though she told herself that it would be for the best in the end.

Even worse, she was deceiving Michael. She dearly hoped he never found out about the *For Better or Worse* agenda. Never did she want him to think that she'd tricked him. She only wanted him to fall in love with her.

Chapter Nine

Michael entered the Barrington Ball with his mother and grandmother, anticipation building inside him. He paused as he realized that truth and pondered the reason behind it. The way he felt had nothing to do with attending a ball but everything to do with who he would see.

Tibby.

There was no other explanation for the tingle of excitement that filled him.

His mother had taken the news of their betrothal well, which had been a relief. She must've witnessed the kiss he and Tibby had shared in the garden the other day. He was pleased they'd taken the time to lay the groundwork for their new relationship.

However, his mother had still remarked about the change in his feelings toward Tibby.

"You've never before shown interest in Tabitha beyond your friendship," she'd said with a puzzled look.

"I suppose I have come to see her in a different light. The qualities that made her a good friend earlier in our lives have deepened my feelings for her."

"What qualities might those be?" she'd asked as if truly curious.

"Her insightfulness for one. To think she suggested I consider writing a mystery..." He was still surprised by that, not to mention flattered that she thought he could. He'd already jotted down some ideas that had come out of nowhere and started re-reading one of his favorite mysteries in an effort to determine how the book was structured.

"That was a surprising suggestion, although I agree with it given how interesting your letters were." She smiled. "I can see the idea intrigues you."

"It does. Botany has been interesting, but writing would be quite different. More consuming, I think." Already he felt more engaged in life and less restless.

Then again, that might have more to do with having Tibby in his world.

"I look forward to hearing more as your ideas take form. Tibby will be thrilled to know she aided you."

"Yes," he agreed. At his mother's expectant look, he continued, "As you already know, she's intelligent and clever as well as loyal and trustworthy." And beautiful, not to mention passionate. He paused, taken aback at where his thoughts were going without urging on his part. The list he'd given his mother had come easily. He really did admire her.

This was a *pretend* betrothal, he reminded himself. No need to go too far in convincing his mother it was real, though he could easily name more reasons he admired Tibby.

"I couldn't agree more," his mother said. "I'm happy for you both and look forward to having her as part of our family. How is Lady Dunford taking the news?"

"Not especially well." He held her gaze. "I was hoping you might be able to help."

"How so?"

"Perhaps encouraging her to attend an event or two. I'm not sure yet. If you have any ideas, I'm certain Tibby would welcome them."

"I do think it's wise of Tibby to press her mother to go out more. It can't aid her physical health or her spirits to stay home all the time." His mother gazed into the distance for a long moment, her expression growing somber. "Too much time alone is rarely good. One's thoughts turn inward."

Michael walked forward to take her hand. "I'm pleased you've adjusted so well to Father's passing."

"I had your grandmother here to prod me out of the doldrums when they struck."

He smiled, easily able to imagine that. "She wouldn't permit either of you to grieve overly long."

"As you know, it's impossible to deny her when she wants something."

Michael had shared the news with his grandmother next.

She'd nodded in approval. "That girl has a head on her shoulders. I think the two of you will make a fine match."

"Thank you, Grandmother. I'm pleased you think so."

"Passion is the secret to a long marriage." She'd winked. "Be certain you're compatible in that way as well."

Michael hadn't known how to respond. Leave it to his grandmother to manage to embarrass him when he'd thought himself beyond such things.

Both his mother and grandmother were in fine spirits this evening. After they finished greeting Lord and Lady Barrington, he offered his arm to each, and they followed the other guests into the ballroom. Finely dressed guests filled the large, elegant space, creating a colorful view.

Chandeliers with hundreds of candles were aided by numerous girandoles along the walls to light the space, all with gold trim. The moon, planets, and shooting stars had been chalked in white on the dance floor to help prevent anyone from slipping. Bouquets of white flowers from roses to lilies to dahlias and more were arranged in gold vases throughout the room.

"This is going to be a crush," his mother whispered with a smile.

"Don't you always say that the best balls are?" Michael asked.

"Of course." She perused the room and settled on someone in the distance. "Escort me to Lady Merriweather." She tipped her head in the direction of her friend. "I am beside myself to share the news of your betrothal."

Somehow, her words were like a punch to his gut. This was it. There was no turning back. Not until a few months had passed when they broke off their association.

"Is all well, my dear?" his grandmother asked when his step faltered.

"Yes, of course. I was just looking for Tibby."

His grandmother's grin suggested he'd given the right answer. "Off with you," she declared as she released his arm. "Your mother and I will be fine on our own."

"Yes, dear," his mother added as she also released him. "Find your Tibby."

Your Tibby.

The longing that stole through him caught him off guard. He forced himself to take a deep breath as his mother and grandmother continued toward their friends.

"You look as if you've been hit by a train." Viscount Garland joined him with a clap on his shoulder a moment later.

"Garland. Good to see you." He shook the man's offered hand.

They'd been acquainted for years, having gotten into a few scrapes together during their time at university.

"Is all well?" Garland asked. He looked much the same as when Michael had last seen him with dark hair and a friendly smile. A title, wealth, and pleasing features surely meant he had his pick of the ladies.

"Indeed." Michael straightened. "I suppose I'm still adjusting to my news." He needed to start sharing the betrothal with others lest his family become concerned.

"What news is that?"

"I'm betrothed." Odd, but he couldn't quite bring himself to say he was to be married. Not when that wasn't the truth.

"Truly?" Garland's brows lifted in surprise. "That was quick. From what I heard you've only just returned to London."

"Yes. It hasn't been long."

"Congratulations. There seems to be a lot of that going around these days."

"Oh?"

"The Earl of Bolton recently married."

"I have yet to see him since my return." He was curious as to how Bolton felt about taking his vows.

Garland leaned closer. "Who will be your bride?"

"Lady Tabitha Malton."

The other man frowned. "I believe I remember her. Wasn't she a neighbor of yours? I'm certain I've heard her name before, though I do my best to avoid attending functions like this."

"Yes. She's a longtime friend."

"You're braver than I to consider tying the knot. Was this a union your parents arranged?"

"No. We renewed our acquaintance upon my return home, and matters progressed from there."

"I wish you happiness." Garland smiled. "If you're available, why don't you swing by the club tomorrow afternoon, and we'll talk more?"

"I'd like that." Michael bid him goodbye and continued his search for Tibby.

It didn't take long for him to see her speaking with friends a short distance away. He took a moment to admire her appearance this evening as she looked especially lovely.

Her emerald-green gown featured a low neckline with a narrow cream-colored ruffle along the edge. The ruffle repeated in tiers along the hemline. Her hair was twisted upward into an elegant coiffure with several strands left unbound to frame her face, making her eyes look even bigger.

Light filled her expression as she spoke with the other ladies, bringing to mind his mother's remark about staying home too often. He need only see the happiness on Tibby's expression to know he was doing the right thing. She needed time with friends, too. Staying home to care for her mother so often wasn't good for either of them.

As if feeling the weight of his regard, Tibby turned and met his gaze, and her face brightened even more. Her obvious joy at seeing him created a lightness in his chest that nearly had him pressing a hand against it.

How interesting to realize that while he'd had the opportunity to see wonderous lands, meet interesting people, gained lifetime friends, and done things he hadn't known he was capable of during his time in the army, none of those experiences compared to this feeling.

A voice inside his head reminded him this wasn't real. At least, it wasn't supposed to be. Still, he found himself walking forward to greet her as if it was. Surely he was just playing the part for her friends. However, the need to name a reason for his actions fell away as he reached for her hand.

"Good evening, Tibby."

"Michael. How nice to see you."

"You look beautiful this evening."

Her eyes widened even as her cheeks grew pink. "Thank you."

He forced his gaze to shift away so he could greet her friends, two of the three he'd met before.

Both ladies watched him with even more curiosity than last time, if that was possible. Did that mean she had told them the news?

"My mother was quite excited to speak with her friends this evening," he began once they'd finished exchanging pleasantries and he had a moment with Tibby while her friends spoke together.

"Oh?" Tibby's brow lifted. "Why is that?"

"She's anxious to tell them of our betrothal."

Tibby's lips parted, her surprise obvious.

Michael was pleased he wasn't the only one to be startled. Could she possibly feel the same way he did, as if this was somehow the point of no return?

"I suppose I thought we would have more time." Her brow puckered with concern.

He leaned close. "Shouldn't we proceed with...everything? Is there a reason to wait?"

"I suppose not." She pressed a hand to her middle, making him wonder at her thoughts.

"But?" He knew her well enough to sense her hesitation.

Her lips tightened, then she whispered, "It just seems like the more people we tell, the more guilt I carry."

That was something he understood completely. "As do I. But keeping it a secret wouldn't serve our purpose."

She heaved a sigh. "You're right, of course." Her gaze sought his. "I know your mother's been suggesting you consider taking a wife, but I don't like to fool her."

Nor did he. "We must think of this as real for the moment. No one need know that it's only temporary."

"Very well."

He could see his words didn't completely reassure her. That was something else they had in common. He wasn't fully certain they were doing the right thing either. However, now wasn't the time or place to reconsider. That moment had passed.

"Shall we stroll around the ballroom?" he asked. They both needed to stop dwelling on doubts. A distraction was needed.

Tibby smiled. "Yes. Victor and Elizabeth are here somewhere, though I've lost track of them."

After a nod at her friends, she took his arm, and they moved slowly around the ballroom.

They hadn't gone far when Tibby stiffened and pulled back on his arm. The look of alarm on her face had him following her gaze to find the cause. Two ladies who looked alike enough to be sisters held Tibby's attention, but he didn't recognize either of them. Still, there was no denying the dismay on Tibby's face. "What is it?"

She smoothed her features and gave a small shake of her head. "Nothing."

He knew it was something. His protective instincts rose like a flag on the battlefield to alert the troops. He might not see the problem, and he was somewhat disappointed that Tibby didn't confide in him, but that wouldn't prevent him from protecting her.

First, he needed to understand the threat.

TIBBY KNEW IT WAS RIDICULOUS to try to avoid Lady Lucinda and her sister, Lady Jane, but conversations with them never went well.

Sharing the news of her 'betrothal' with Harriet and Frances was one thing. Sharing it with the two sisters was another matter entirely and one for which she wasn't prepared. Especially not after what they'd done to her friend, Phoebe, after Lady Lucinda had overheard Phoebe and Frances speaking about the literary league's secret agenda.

Panic struck and she tried to guide Michael in the opposite direction of the ladies.

Much to her chagrin, he planted his feet and looked down at her. "There is nothing we can't overcome together."

The urge to scoff nearly overcame her. Had he forgotten that none of this was real? Did he need to be reminded of that?

She stared at him with dismay, only to note the sincerity of his expression. The way he held her gaze with such confidence and affection caught her breath. But it was affection between friends, she reminded herself. Nothing more. She couldn't expect his feelings to have changed this quickly.

"Let us weather the storm together," he murmured. Then he escorted her forward, still looking into her eyes as if she were the only person in the room who mattered.

"Lady Tabitha, how surprising to see you here this evening," Lady Lucinda said.

"You so rarely attend balls," Lady Jane added.

Tibby wrenched her gaze from Michael to greet the two ladies. "Good evening." Did she bother to address their comments?

Lady Lucinda looked over Michael from head to toe as if she were a cat and he a tasty morsel on a plate. "I don't think I've had the pleasure of being introduced to your companion." The lady glanced between them, her curiosity obvious. "Is he your cousin?"

The barb struck Tibby. How clever of Lady Lucinda to suggest Michael wouldn't be bothered with Tibby unless they were related.

"Nothing of the sort," Michael responded with a charming smile. "Lady Tabitha and I have been...*friends* for some time." The emphasis he placed on the term suggested so much more.

So much more that it—and his gaze—made Tibby shiver.

She made the introductions but couldn't bring herself to claim Michael as her fiancé. His questioning look weighed on her as he spoke with the sisters. Still, Tibby couldn't force the words past her lips, worried the pair would immediately see through the lie.

"Can you ladies keep a secret?" Michael asked the sisters.

Tibby stared at him in astonishment. No, they couldn't. Their propensity for gossip was what made them unliked by the entire literary league. Not just gossip, but the mean-spirited kind.

Lady Lucinda shared an excited look with her sister. "Of course, we can."

Tibby pressed her lips firmly together before the word "liar" escaped.

"Lady Tabitha and I have recently become betrothed." Michael grinned as if he were the happiest man on earth. "You're among the first to know."

The sisters swung their gazes in unison to Tibby, clearly unable to believe the news could be true.

A hot flush of embarrassment filled Tibby's cheeks. This was a disaster. How had she thought she could pretend to be betrothed when it was impossible for anyone to believe it? Michael was charismatic and handsome while she was just...Tibby. Plain, awkward Tibby who no one bothered to look at twice.

Even now, Lady Lucinda's eyes widened. "C—congratulations, Lady Tabitha." She looked at Michael again. "Congratulations to you both."

A look of what appeared to be longing flashed across the woman's face. Tibby recognized it, for she'd felt the same way more times than she could count.

"We wish you much happiness," Lady Jane added with a wistful smile.

To Tibby's surprise, they both seemed to think her reaction was natural rather than because she was pretending. "Thank you," she managed.

"If you'll excuse us, Lady Tabitha has promised me a dance." With that, Michael led her toward the dance floor. "That wasn't so bad, was it?" he asked.

"No, it wasn't." Perhaps this was going to work after all.

She only wished she could ask him not to look at her as if she mattered more than anything to him. If she wasn't careful, she'd start to believe it.

Chapter Ten

"Good afternoon, Shaw." Viscount Garland rose to shake Michael's hand at the club the following afternoon.

"Garland. I see you survived the ball without issue."

The viscount chuckled as he gestured toward a chair at the table. "Yes, but I'm hoping not to repeat the experience any time soon."

Michael was in fine spirits. He'd spent the morning jotting down notes on a potential story idea that seemed promising. Writing a mystery would be challenging, but one he looked forward to.

He'd slept well last night. The few times he'd woke, he shifted his thoughts away from painful memories and instead mulled over ideas for his mystery. That had proven quite effective in calming his usual restlessness.

Well, thoughts on the book, as well as those of Tibby, he amended. Her suggestion of pretending to be betrothed had certainly changed how he thought of her, and her recommendation that he write a book had continued that path.

How was it that she knew him better than he'd realized, yet he didn't feel as if he knew her in the same fashion? She surprised him at every turn, making him wonder what she might say or do next.

"I would think all the looks cast your way by the ladies would be flattering." Michael signaled for the waiter.

Garland gave a mock shudder. "Not when I know what they truly want."

"Are you certain you don't wish to marry? Or is it that you haven't found a lady who has caught your interest?"

"My interest, perhaps, but not my affection." Garland held his gaze for a long moment, his expression unreadable. "Not like you have."

Michael hesitated on how to respond. He'd been playing a part last evening during the ball. How could he not continue to do so after seeing Tibby's upset caused by the conversation with the two sisters?

"Don't deny it," Garland said after they'd ordered their drinks. "I saw the way you looked at Lady Tabitha. You two are clearly in love."

Michael did his best to hide his surprise. "I have known her for a long time. Since childhood."

Garland leaned forward with elbows on the table. "What changed? How did you know?"

She suggested we pretend to be betrothed. He couldn't share that. He searched his mind for an explanation that would sound plausible. "I suppose I saw a different side of her I hadn't noticed. As if I didn't know her as well as I thought I did." He still didn't.

"Hmm. You should definitely speak with the Earl of Bolton, for you seem to have much in common from what he told me." Garland took a sip of his whisky. "Enough of women and marriage. Tell me of your adventures. How did you find New Zealand?"

Though Michael had little desire to speak of his time in the military, it was preferable to his complicated feelings for Tibby.

When he'd realized how uncomfortable she was when he'd pressed her to share their betrothal with Lady Lucinda and Lady Jane, his chest had tightened. If she couldn't share the news, how was she ever going to endure the questions and comments she'd receive when she broke it off?

Or did she expect to withdraw from Society at that point and remain home, taking care of her mother?

They needed to speak further on the topic, so he understood her plan. Perhaps they could create a valid excuse together that suited her.

He pulled his thoughts back to Garland's question. "New Zealand is a beautiful country. Rugged and untamed. The wildlife is unique."

"And Australia?"

"A different world entirely, though I saw only a small portion of it." Michael nodded toward Garland. "What of you? I'm certain you had your own adventures in the time I've been gone."

"A few," he admitted with a smile only to quickly sober. "Though my father would prefer I have none."

"I hoped that perhaps the situation had improved." Michael remembered all too well Garland recounting some of the disagreements he'd had with his overly strict father.

"Not at all. He still quotes Bible verses as if they are imprinted on his soul and frequently threatens to disinherit me for my foul behavior."

"That can't be easy to endure." Michael knew that when the viscount was younger, he'd been deprived of food and water for days when his father had found fault. Garland had moved from home immediately after university.

"I would walk away and never see him again if it weren't for Mother."

Michael drew a slow breath at the reminder of her. The woman had been little more than a shadow the last time he'd seen her. She wasn't allowed to stand at her husband's side, only behind him. Her mission in life was to remain as invisible as possible, both to her husband and any onlookers.

That had to be impossible for her son to watch, yet Michael knew Garland wouldn't abandon her completely to his father's strange ideas.

"I wish I knew a way to help." Michael waited to see if Garland would say more. He didn't think many knew how terrible the situation was or how deeply it affected the viscount. He let few people know his true self. That was something to which Michael could relate as he had his share of secrets he had no intention of telling anyone.

"As do I." Garland stared into his drink for a long moment before lifting his gaze to meet Michael's. "It sounds terrible, but I wish he were dead."

"I don't blame you." From what little Michael knew, it seemed the only way the situation would change.

Garland had already tried numerous tactics from pleading with his father to threatening him to quoting Bible verses back to him. Nothing swayed the earl from his opinion that he acted as a true Christian gentleman should and that no one else did, including his son.

Michael's frustration with his mother's continual comments about finding a wife now felt petty. Still, he refused to allow Tibby's situation to become more dire than it already was. Helping her by pretending they were engaged was the right thing to do. It wasn't hurting anyone and might aid Tibby and Lady Dunford.

Whether he wanted it to end any time soon was a question for another day. Surely, it wasn't wrong to enjoy the pleasurable moments with Tibby. Worry over the future could wait a few more weeks.

TIBBY PAUSED OUTSIDE the closed door of her mother's bedroom and took a moment to gather her defenses. She had been very displeased that Tibby had gone to the ball and made that displeasure known from the moment she'd woken.

In all honesty, Tibby hadn't realized how difficult a pretend betrothal with Michael would be to carry out. Misleading friends and family wasn't easy, and regret was a heavier burden than she'd expected. The continued reminders to herself that it wouldn't be a lie if she were able to convince Michael they were the perfect match didn't alleviate her worry.

But how did she protect her heart when he was being so caring and believable in his role as her fiancé? That was another element she hadn't fully considered. Instead, she'd only looked forward to being with him. Each time they were together, her feelings for him grew. What she felt now was so different than before—richer and deeper.

With so many conflicting emotions tumbling through her, it was difficult to enjoy their time together.

Telling herself to enjoy them no longer seemed wise—not when she feared for her heart.

She shifted the tea tray and tapped on the door before opening it. "I brought tea, Mother," she announced with a cheery smile.

Her mother had remained in bed all day, adding to Tibby's guilt. However, the sight of her propped against the pillows looking healthy despite her protests otherwise also filled Tibby with frustration.

Was it so much to ask that her mother think of someone other than herself for a change?

"You needn't have bothered," her mother replied then heaved a sigh. "I don't know that I feel up to having tea." She tugged at the bed linens to tuck them more firmly around her.

"Nonsense." Tibby rounded the bed with the tray, keeping her smile in place. "Cook made some of the little frosted cakes you like. I thought we might read while we have our tea."

"Are you certain you have time to spend with me?" Her mother glanced out the window. "I thought perhaps you and Captain Shaw had plans for the afternoon."

Her mother had always called Michael by his given name until she'd learned of their betrothal. Then he'd suddenly become Captain Shaw.

Tibby took a firmer hold on her patience. "Not this afternoon." She didn't know when she might see Michael again. They hadn't determined the next steps for their plan as of yet. She'd been tempted to visit his greenhouse this morning with the hope of seeing him, but with her mother in such low spirits, she'd decided it was best not to.

She set the tray on the bedside table and pulled the chair closer. Then she poured her mother a cup and added a spoonful of sugar and a dash of milk before handing her the cup. "Would you like some cake first or shall I read?"

"It doesn't matter. Do what you like. You always do."

Tibby clenched her jaw to hold back a sharp retort. She was beginning to doubt she had enough patience to deal with the situation without speaking her mind. Ignoring her mother certainly wasn't doing any good.

Tibby read for nearly a half hour, taking breaks to sip her tea and keeping a watchful eye on her mother. The story was engaging, and as always, reading lifted her mood and allowed her to set aside her own problems, however briefly, and replace them with someone else's. Escaping was one of the many reasons she enjoyed the pastime.

At last, she inserted a bookmark at the end of a chapter and set aside the book. "Shall we have some cake?" she asked her mother.

"I suppose, though I'm not particularly hungry."

The urge to simply take the tray and leave was nearly overwhelming. There was no pleasing her mother when she was like this.

Tibby ignored her remark once again, served the cake, and then refilled their cups. Yet as they sat in silence, it became impossible for Tibby not to share some of her feelings.

"I realize you're not pleased about my betrothal," she began. She still couldn't bring herself to mention an upcoming wedding when it seemed so doubtful that would ever come to pass. "But I hope you can come to terms with it and try to be happy for me."

"I shouldn't be surprised that you plan to leave me, too." Her mother kept her gaze fixed straight ahead, her lips pressed tight.

"I'm not leaving you," Tibby said, despite the prick of her conscience. "Besides, I don't think it's good for you to stay home so much. It's not good for either of us. We need to enjoy friends and activities."

"You only say that because you'll soon be leaving."

"Mother, that is not true. I won't be far away. Whether I'm here or not, you should have your own friends and interests. Haven't you been lonely since father died?"

"Of course, I have. But how can I enjoy anything without him?"

"I miss him too. It's difficult not to have him with us when we did so much together. But spending every day alone or with me isn't what he would want, nor does it make you happy."

"You don't see the way people look at me." Her mother sniffed. "They don't want to be around me any more than I want to be near them."

"Perhaps if you made more of an effort at making conversation," Tibby suggested. "Speaking only of your illnesses is rather depressing." She watched her mother carefully, wondering if she'd gone too far. Perhaps she should've waited to speak with her so bluntly until Victor was here. Yet then her mother would only accuse them of joining forces against her.

"So I'm to lie and say I'm fine when asked?" Her mother looked affronted at the thought.

"Sometimes. People don't know how to react when you continually speak about your ailments." Especially when she looked healthy enough.

"If people truly cared, they'd offer sympathy."

"When they do, you tend to list even more problems, Mother." Tibby's exasperation loosened her tongue. "Do you even remember to ask others how they are? Or what's happening in their lives?"

Her mouth dropped open in outrage. "I know how to carry on a conversation, Tabitha. Thank you very much. I certainly don't need to be reminded by you."

"If not me, then who?" Tibby's voice shook with emotion as she scooted to the edge of her chair, prepared to push harder with the hope she could get through to her. "None of your friends call anymore. I don't want you to live in isolation."

"Do you even like Captain Shaw, or is he just a convenient way to escape me?"

"I'm not trying to escape. I'm trying to have a life." A lump filled Tibby's throat at the admission. A life with Michael, preferably. But she wouldn't confess that when more than likely, her hope would soon end. "I'm not leaving you, Mother."

"Forgive me, but I have difficulty believing that when you latched on to the first man to cross your path."

Tibby rose, her body stiff as hurt flooded her. "If you insist on speaking so unkindly, I must assume you would prefer your own company over mine."

Though she longed to slam the door on her way out, she shut it quietly instead. Why did she bother to try so hard with her mother when she so clearly wanted to remain in her unhappy world?

The urge to speak with someone about all this rushed in. The thought of speaking to Michael propelled her down the stairs and out to the garden. While it seemed unfair to burden him with her upset, he had seen firsthand how difficult her mother could be.

Phoebe was away, enjoying her honeymoon. Tibby could speak with Harriet or Frances, but she'd never told them of the extent of her mother's behavior.

In many ways, it was embarrassing that Tibby had allowed her mother's feigned illnesses to guide her life the way they had. If only she were stronger and could find a way to make her see reason.

Instead, she'd allowed one day to turn into the next. First days passed, then weeks, months, and now years, all with Tibby trying to endure her mother's poor moods and feigned illnesses.

Thank goodness she'd taken a step away, even if it was pretend. Otherwise, she'd be as isolated as her mother. Already it was a rare occurrence to visit with friends other than at league meetings.

Her steps flew along the garden path to the gate in the fence. Though it seemed unlikely that Michael was in the greenhouse, she had to try.

She'd only taken a few steps when she heard her name. If she hadn't been in such a state of upset, she would've seen Lady Trafford tending one of her rose beds, wearing her wide-brimmed garden hat.

"Good afternoon, Lady Trafford." Tibby clasped her hands before her, trying to calm. "I'm terribly sorry to intrude. I thought perhaps Michael was in the greenhouse."

"He's at his club at the moment." Lady Trafford's sympathetic gaze held on her as if she sensed her troubled mood. "I'm not sure how long he'll be. Is there anything I can assist you with?"

Tibby managed a smile. "It's nothing important."

"Are you certain?" She lifted a brow, the gesture reminding Tibby of Michael. "Forgive me, but I can see you're distressed. If there's anything I can do to help..."

Tibby pressed a finger to her brow as the temptation to speak warred within her. It felt disloyal to talk about her mother with Lady Trafford even though she was fairly certain the lady had already witnessed her mother's behavior for herself.

"It has been a trying day." Tibby glanced over her shoulder at her house, blinking back tears. "I thought it would be nice to speak to Michael."

"Your mother is...unwell today?"

"One might say that." Unwell in spirits. Not in health.

Lady Trafford rose and stepped closer. "Tabitha, I didn't fully realize the extent of your mother's state until recently. I'm sorry I didn't try to intervene earlier."

"Oh, please." Tibby shook her head. "You did. On numerous occasions. You called frequently and invited her to various functions. What more could you have done?"

"I should've kept trying. Your mother and I used to be such good friends. I miss her."

Tibby missed the way her mother used to be as well. She was ashamed to say that there were times when she didn't care for the lady who'd taken her place. "Thank you for all the times you tried." Tibby lifted a hand only to let it fall and released a shuddering breath. "I'm not sure what else to do to encourage her to rejoin life."

The lady nodded. "I wish I had a suggestion." She studied Tibby for a long moment "Perhaps once she adjusts to the news of your...betrothal, she will be forced to reconsider her options."

Tibby's gaze flew to Lady Trafford's, her heart in her throat. Something in the way the lady looked at her made Tibby fear she knew the truth—that their supposed betrothal was nothing but a ruse. And that it had all been Tibby's idea.

Chapter Eleven

M*ay I take you for a ride in Hyde Park this afternoon? If so, wave from the drawing room window.*

M

Tibby smiled, her mood lifting at Michael's invitation. The message arrived soon after she'd finished breakfast and made her feel as if perhaps all *was* right with the world. That was a welcome sensation.

Surely, she'd worried for no reason after her conversation with his mother. If Lady Trafford suspected the betrothal was anything but real, wouldn't she have said something? The lady was unfailingly kind but often direct. Tibby's guilt had been what made her think his mother was suspicious.

As for her own mother, Tibby feared she wouldn't be able to convince her to step out of the house despite her best efforts. She wasn't ready to give up by any means but didn't know what more she could do.

The concern could wait for another day, she decided, as she left her bedroom and hurried to the drawing room. A glance out the window showed Michael near the garden fence, looking directly up at her.

Her heart somersaulted at the sight of him. Oh dear. She was in serious trouble. Yet how could she guard her heart against falling in love when he was so appealing? He was handsome, confident, attentive, and the way he looked at her made her feel wanted. The list could go on. Not to mention the passion in their last kiss.

She was torn between wanting another and hoping there weren't anymore. She squeezed her eyes shut briefly. Who was she kidding? Of course, she wanted another.

Tibby waggled her fingers at him, and he returned the gesture and smiled. With a brief bow, he turned and strode back to his house. She watched him go, wondering not for the first time if it was habit that had him walking so quickly everywhere he went.

She turned away from the window with a sigh, already wishing the afternoon was here. Any time with Michael would be wonderful but a ride in Hyde Park, something a normal betrothed couple might do, sounded particularly appealing.

"Lady Tabitha?"

She looked up to see Alice standing in the doorway, concern on her face. The look filled Tibby with trepidation. "Yes?"

"Lady Dunford doesn't seem to be feeling well."

Tibby frowned. That wasn't anything out of the ordinary.

"She seems to be running a fever," Alice continued.

"Truly?" Surprise gripped Tibby. During her mother's numerous claims to be unwell, never had she had a fever. Her symptoms were never measurable or visible.

"She's awake if you'd like to see for yourself." Alice frowned, clearly worried. "I wouldn't have noticed anything unusual except her cheeks are flushed and her eyes look a bit glassy."

Regret weighed on Tibby's heart. Had what she'd said the previous day contributed to her mother feeling poorly? She gave herself a mental shake at the ridiculous notion and followed Alice to her mother's bedroom.

Her mother's eyes were closed though she was propped up against the pillows, a plain cotton nightcap pulled over her hair. Her cheeks were indeed flushed.

Tibby drew nearer to the bed. "Good morning, Mother." She smiled when her mother opened her eyes.

"Tibby." She blinked several times then pulled the covers up to her chin. "I'm chilled."

"I'll fetch another blanket, my lady," Alice offered.

Tibby sat on the edge of the bed. "How are you feeling?" Though she normally avoided the question as it only encouraged her mother to list her ailments, based on her appearance, it was necessary.

The glare her mother cast her couldn't be missed. "According to you, I should simply say I'm well."

"Mother. Please." Tibby placed a hand on her flushed cheek, dismayed to find it burning. "I can clearly see something is amiss. You're overly warm to the touch."

The older woman heaved a sigh. "My head aches as does my body." She gave a small cough. "My throat is uncomfortable as well."

"I'm sorry to hear that. Why don't I consult with the cook and see if we can prepare a warm, soothing drink for you?"

"I wouldn't want to be a bother."

"You're not a bother." Tibby was careful not to say *never*. That would be a lie, and she'd told enough of those of late. "I'm happy to do it."

She waited for Alice to return with a blanket then departed for the kitchen to consult with Cook. Tibby enjoyed preparing medicinal remedies with the herbs she grew but was far from an expert. Cook, on the other hand, knew more than Tibby could ever hope to.

A brief discussion had them steeping some mint in steaming water with ginger and honey.

"It sounds like nothing more than a bit of a cold, my lady," Cook reassured her. "She'll be feeling more the thing in a day or two."

"I hope so." Tibby carried the tray up the stairs, reassured by her words.

Her mother sipped some of the tea and immediately fell back asleep.

Tibby kept watch over her while she worked on some embroidery, hoping she'd wake feeling better.

A quiet tap on the door had her looking up to see Alice.

The maid came forward to whisper, "Captain Shaw is calling. Shall I watch Lady Dunford for a time?"

"Oh, dear." Tibby had forgotten Michael's invitation in her concern for her mother. "Yes, please. I'll return as soon as I speak with him."

Disappointment flooded her. Her mother's illness had poor timing, not that any illness came at a convenient time. She went to the drawing room and found Michael waiting for her by the window.

He turned to her with a smile. "Good afternoon, Tibby." His smile faded quickly when he took in her expression. "What is it?"

"My apologies, but I won't be able to accompany you after all. Mother is running a fever." Tibby waited for him to question the validity of her illness, but he didn't. How kind of him.

"I'm sorry to hear that. I hope it's nothing serious."

"As do I."

Michael walked forward to take her hands, surprising her. After all, no one watched that they needed to convince of their new relationship since they were alone. "I won't say I'm not disappointed, because I am."

Her heart did a slow roll in her chest. "I am as well. It looks like a lovely day for it."

"You're truly worried, aren't you?" he asked quietly.

"Yes. Though she frequently complains of ills and aches, she rarely has any visible symptoms like this."

"Don't allow this to change our plan, Tibby." He released her hand to briefly cradle her cheek, his touch welcome. "You deserve a life of your own. That doesn't mean you won't be there for her when she needs you."

She nodded, realizing how comforting his words were. He really did know her well if he realized how worried she was. "I'll keep that in mind."

"Let me know if there's anything I can do. Or my mother. She'd be happy to help as well."

The memory of her conversation with Lady Trafford came to mind. "Has your mother said anything further about our betrothal?"

"Such as what?" His eyes narrowed with confusion.

"Never mind. I suppose I was just curious how she felt about it."

"She's happy for us." He shook his head. "In truth, that only makes me feel guiltier."

Tibby bit her lip. "This is harder than I expected."

"It is." The understanding in his eyes eased her worry. "However, that doesn't change the reasons we are doing this. To help ourselves and your mother."

"Yes, you're right." But she couldn't release her doubts completely. She glanced over her shoulder. "I should return to Mother."

"Of course." Michael squeezed her hand. "I'll be thinking of you." He held her gaze before his focus dropped to her mouth.

For just a moment, she thought he might kiss her. Hope flared inside her. Then the moment was gone, and she was certain she'd only imagined it. At times, it was difficult to remember that they were pretending. The lines blurred in her mind far too often.

After his departure, she returned to her mother's side. The remainder of the day was a long one. Her mother's fever didn't improve. If anything, it worsened. Nothing she or Alice did seemed to bring it down. Still, they continued to place cool cloths on her forehead with the hope they would help.

They took turns watching over their patient. But when Tibby wasn't with her mother, she worried. When night fell, she sent Alice to bed and dozed fitfully in a chair beside her mother next to the bed.

Just after midnight, her mother started to cough. It worsened steadily until her mother's lungs rattled with every breath she took. As soon as dawn lit the sky, Tibby sent for the doctor.

She also sent a message to Victor, wanting him to be aware of their mother's condition. She took a moment to look out her mother's bedroom window, where she could just see the roofline of Trafford House. Was Michael sleeping? Or had he woken early to work on his book? She wished she knew and dearly hoped to see him soon.

Dr. Hackett came within the hour, much to her relief. He'd been their physician for as long as Tibby could remember. The tall, thin man with grey whiskers and a somber countenance seemed concerned about her mother as well, which only added to Tibby's worry.

"Lady Dunford's high fever is troubling," he advised after briefly examining her. "The congestion deep in her lungs is of even more concern."

"We've tried a few remedies," Tibby advised, "but none of them seem to provide relief."

"I will leave laudanum for the cough but use it cautiously." The physician also left instructions to send for him if Lady Dunford didn't improve in the next two days.

His visit did little to reassure Tibby. Victor's reply only asked her to keep him informed when possible. She didn't find that helpful either.

After another long day, her mother's condition was no better. Tibby applied a mustard plaster on her chest to aid her cough, careful to only leave it on for twenty minutes to avoid blistering. The laudanum helped slightly, but it was difficult to convince her mother to take it. Tibby remained at her bedside all night once again.

By the next morning, Tibby had grown even more concerned and sent for the doctor once more. Dr. Hackett provided a tincture of belladonna for her cough but had no additional suggestions, much to her dismay.

She sent another note to Victor, suggesting he visit soon as Tibby was no longer certain whether her mother would survive another night.

Alice checked on Tibby frequently, offering to relieve her, but Tibby sent her to bed. She couldn't possibly leave her mother's side when she was doing so poorly.

Remorse filled her for their argument and her selfish wish to ease away from her mother. What kind of daughter even considered such a thing? She'd made a terrible mistake by suggesting the pretend betrothal.

The sky lightened with the coming of dawn, and Tibby rose to place another cool cloth on her mother's forehead, hoping it would provide some comfort. As she adjusted the cloth, her mother opened her eyes, much to her surprise. The glassy, heavy-lidded look of them was anything but comforting.

"Tibby, I'm so pleased you're here." The words were barely audible, and Tibby leaned close to better hear her. "What would I ever do without you?" she whispered.

Tibby's heart clutched. "Don't speak, Mother. You should rest. Would you like a sip of water?"

Her mother nodded weakly, and Tibby assisted her with a drink. Tibby hoped that was a good sign.

One thing was clear. She couldn't continue to pretend to be betrothed to Michael. Not when her mother depended on her. It seemed apparent that the worry of Tibby leaving home had contributed to her mother's illness.

Thank goodness they hadn't told many people about the supposed betrothal. That would make it easier to end without much fuss.

Despite her decision, a voice deep inside her rebelled. She looked around the dimly lit bedroom. Was this to be her future if she gave up on her plan? To always be near her mother in case she was needed?

She gave herself a mental shake. Such selfish thoughts were not who she was. Besides, she loved her mother. The situation could be much worse. She still had her friends and the literary league and maybe, just maybe, she could convince her mother to venture out on occasion.

The quiet sigh of longing that escaped surprised her. Now wasn't the time for self-pity. Her mother needed her. Tibby intended to be there for her.

She settled into her chair again, relieved when her mother fell into a sound sleep. Tibby dozed fitfully, trying to determine how she'd find the courage to tell Michael. How ironic that it seemed she needed even more courage than when she'd first suggested the idea to him.

Alice came to take her place two hours later. Tibby rose and placed a gentle hand on her mother's forehead, relieved to note her fever had eased.

"That's an excellent sign, my lady," Alice said. "Such a relief. Why don't you get some rest, and I'll watch over her?"

Tibby nodded. "Please wake me if her condition changes."

"Of course. She seems to be sleeping much better than before."

"I hope it means she's on the mend." With a grateful nod at Alice, Tibby went to her bedroom and slept fully clothed, too exhausted to change.

MICHAEL FOUND HIMSELF staring out the drawing room window toward Dunford House once again, something he'd done far more often than he should over the past few days. He'd spent time working in the greenhouse as well as working on ideas for the mystery, but it was difficult to concentrate when his thoughts remained on Tibby.

The morning was growing long, but he couldn't bring himself to leave his post.

He had learned from the footman who was friends with Tibby's maid that Lady Dunford was giving them all a scare. Her condition continued to worsen, and everyone was worried.

It came as no surprise when Michael saw Victor's carriage pull up before Dunford House and he and his wife alighted, their expressions somber.

That only made Michael worry more about how Tibby was faring even if he was relieved her brother had come to lend support in whatever form he could.

Michael managed to wait until the afternoon to ask the footman to discover what he could from the maid. He didn't want to bother Tibby by sending a message which would require her to take the time to reply.

He knew exactly what path Tibby's thoughts would take after this. She would want to break off their betrothal.

Michael could understand her reasoning, especially since Lady Dunford was so ill. However, he intended to do everything he could to convince Tibby otherwise. He didn't believe for a moment that their betrothal had anything to do with Lady Dunford's illness.

In his opinion, the situation hadn't changed. Tibby still needed a way to gain the chance for a future, and he intended to help in every way he could. Hopefully, the situation would make Victor realize how dependent his mother had become on Tibby. That wasn't fair. Tibby deserved more.

While he knew she would always be involved in her mother's life, she needed the chance to have one of her own. She deserved that and so much more. If he could help her find it, he would.

"Good news, Captain," the footman began upon his return. "Her ladyship's fever has broken, and they believe she will soon recover. Lady Tabitha was even able to convince her to drink some broth."

Michael blew out a relieved breath. The last thing he wanted was for Lady Dunford's condition to worsen, which would've left Tibby with guilt too heavy to bear.

He managed to keep his patience until the next morning before sending a message to Tibby.

Meet me in the greenhouse this morning if you can.

M

He'd been dawdling in the greenhouse for well over an hour before the sound of the door opening had him turning with hope. The sight of Tibby in the doorway made his knees weaken.

"Tibby." The depth of his reaction to her sent him off balance. He'd missed her even more than he'd realized. His thoughts faded as he took in her pale face and the shadows under her eyes. She looked exhausted. He strode forward to take her hands in his. "How is Lady Dunford?" he asked.

"Weak, of course. But slowly improving."

"I'm so pleased to hear that." He shook his head. "I've requested so many updates from our footman that I fear he is considering leaving our employ."

Tibby's smile lifted his heart. "I do believe the maid was flattered until she realized he only wanted updates on Mother."

"How are you faring?" he asked, keeping hold of her hands when she would have pulled away.

He ran the pad of his thumb over her knuckles, grateful she hadn't worn gloves. The physical contact somehow eased his worry for her.

"I'm well." He lifted a brow at the obvious lie. Again she smiled. "A little tired perhaps but very relieved."

"I can only imagine." He released one of her hands to tuck a strand of her hair behind her ear. She looked frail and delicate, almost as if she were the one who'd been ill.

"I thought we might lose her at one point." The tremor in her voice spoke of how worried she'd been.

"How terrifying."

"It was." She nodded, the stark look of fear on her face tugging at him.

Michael drew her into his arms and held her tight, unable to think of another way to comfort her. She remained stiff for a moment then relaxed and leaned her head against his chest.

After a time, he eased back to look at her. All thought fell away in an instant. Unable to resist, he pressed his lips to hers.

To his great pleasure, Tibby lifted her hands to rest on his shoulders and returned the kiss. Passion grew, and he held her against his length, wanting to feel every inch of her.

He ignored the voice inside his head that demanded to know what he was doing. He had no answer. He only wanted the kiss to continue.

Even as he prepared to deepen it, Tibby pulled back. "Michael—"

He placed a finger on her lips, already knowing what she intended to say. "Not yet."

Her brow furrowed with confusion.

"I know you think we should end our betrothal." He removed his finger and adjusted his hold on her, unwilling to set her free just yet. "I disagree."

Tibby shook her head. "My idea was a terrible one, and I'm sorry to have dragged you into it."

"No, it wasn't. And you have nothing to be sorry for. You've come this far. Don't give up now."

"How can I continue this ruse with her feeling so poorly?"

"Because you deserve to have a future of your own. Whatever that entails."

"Not at the cost of my mother's health."

"This is for her own good in the long term. You've said she isn't happy as things are." He could see he had yet to convince her. "At the very least, wait a few days to see how things unfold."

Her heavy sigh suggested she was considering his request.

"Need I remind you that we are doing this on my behalf as well?"

She smiled. "I'm fairly certain your mother would relent if you told her how you feel."

"I have, to no avail."

"Truly?" Her narrowed eyes suggested she didn't believe him.

"Truly." It was mostly true. "Now then, are we in agreement?"

Her lips twisted as she further considered his request. "For now."

How odd that her agreement provided him with such relief.

Chapter Twelve

Michael waited two days before sending another message to Tibby, hoping that by now her mother was well on the mend.

According to his footman, Lady Dunford's sister had arrived from Bath and was staying with them for an extended period of time to help with the lady's recovery.

That had to be a relief to Tibby. Michael would hazard a guess that the aunt had arrived at Lord Dunford's request. He hoped Tibby's brother understood how much of a burden the situation was on his sister.

Michael had given much thought to his actions the last time he'd seen Tibby. Holding her was one thing, for his sympathy was engaged. But that kiss was an entirely different matter, and he had yet to name the reason he'd done it. Surely compassion for her and her plight had been behind his behavior.

He shoved aside the question about why he was so determined not to end their betrothal. Tibby needed help, and he would provide it. That was all. Now that Tibby's aunt had arrived, it could provide an additional way to have her mother less dependent on Tibby.

After much pondering, he decided she wouldn't want to leave the house for long. Not until her mother had made a complete recovery. With that in mind, he thought a picnic in the garden was the perfect solution and something a betrothed couple might enjoy.

He sent a message to Tibby in the morning, hoping she would accept his invitation. To his delight, she answered promptly in the affirmative.

Stokes had the footmen carry a low table out to the garden and set it for a casual yet elegant meal. They could sit on the ground and not have the fuss of a formal luncheon.

Though Michael had previously gone out of his way to make certain his mother saw that first kiss, now he found a sheltered spot that wasn't visible from either house unless someone ventured to one of the bedrooms and looked out.

He hoped his surprise pleased Tibby and would allow her to set aside her worries for a time. When the voice inside his head suggested he had other motivations as well, he ignored it. This was for Tibby, his friend, who'd been through a difficult week.

The time for the picnic couldn't arrive quickly enough as far as he was concerned. The weather was perfect—a warm day with only a few clouds overhead and no hint of rain. He studied the table with a critical eye and decided to gather a small bouquet of flowers to add to it. When had he become a man who picked flowers for a woman? The question was puzzling.

He'd just placed them in a glass when Tibby walked toward him.

"What is all this?" she asked as she took in the white tablecloth and flowers on the table.

"A picnic to take your mind off recent events." He gestured toward the blanket on the ground that would protect her clothing and offer some padding. "Would you care to join me?"

She looked thinner and still tired with smudges beneath her eyes. But when her face lit with pleasure, easing the worry evident in the taut lines of her face, he called his mission a success though it had only begun.

"How thoughtful." Tibby smiled as she sat at his side with the table before them. "You did all this for me?"

"Of course. You deserve something special after all you've been through."

The stunned pleasure on her expression caused his heart to pound more rapidly, and he was doubly pleased he'd made an effort.

A footman brought a pitcher of lemonade and poured them each a glass.

"Oh, my." Tibby smiled as she took hers. "I feel completely spoiled."

"After the worry you endured, you should have someone fuss over you. How is Lady Dunford by now?"

"Improving daily. The visit from Aunt Eleanor has cheered her considerably."

"I'm relieved to hear that."

"Her visit has cheered me, too. Having someone to counter Mother's comments is a relief. Perhaps she'll be better able to improve Mother's spirits than I have managed."

"It's time for someone other than you to have a turn. That much I know for certain."

The footman returned with a tray of chicken croquettes and a tangy cucumber salad, the perfect picnic luncheon.

"What have you been doing over the last few days?" Tibby asked as they served themselves after the footman had departed.

"I visited with a few friends. Worked in the greenhouse." His gaze held hers. "And put together some ideas for a mystery novel."

Tibby set her plate on the low table and reached for his arm. The excitement shining in her brown eyes warmed him. "I'm so pleased to hear that. How are you feeling about it?"

"It's been...interesting thus far. More than I had expected."

Her grin made him smile in return. "Excellent. I was certain you'd enjoy it, even if you only write as a hobby. But I confess I would like to see you publish a book or two."

"I have yet to decide how far to take it. I need to see if I'm any good at creating a story first."

"You will be," she replied with a single nod. "I have no doubt."

"Your faith in my skills could very well be misplaced." He waited, hoping she disagreed. His doubt was unexpected, something he rarely experienced. But writing felt so new and different.

He'd never before pursued a creative endeavor. While in the army, his agenda for each day had been black and white. His duties had certainly been challenging and sometimes unpleasant, but they hadn't required him to use his imagination.

Did he even have one? Would he be skilled at this? He wasn't sure he liked feeling so out of his element, like a fish flopping about on the shore, uncertain how to find its way back to the water.

"If writing stories was easy, more people would consider doing it." Tibby popped the last of her croquette into her mouth and chewed slowly as if savoring the flavor. "Testing oneself can be intimidating. But if we never did so, how would we grow?"

He pondered her words as the footman returned with another course. The idea of trying something new and unfamiliar was appealing in many ways. It had already helped to take his thoughts off the terrible memories of events during his military career.

Yet he couldn't deny that he was nervous about failing.

The confidence that shone in Tibby's eyes filled him with a mix of emotions. Her faith was humbling. She had always believed in him, even when they were little more than children.

What had he done to deserve a friend like her? No—not merely a friend. She was much more special than that.

As always, his thoughts skittered away from defining his feelings. That didn't mean he couldn't appreciate their relationship.

"If only I had the same faith in myself that you have," he said with a smile.

"Have no fear. I have enough for both of us."

His heart rolled over in his chest at her words, and it was all he could do not to press a hand to it. Thank goodness Tibby hadn't broken off their betrothal or this moment wouldn't be happening.

"May I ask a question?" Her serious expression made him wonder if he should deny her request.

"Of course," he reluctantly agreed, hoping she wouldn't bring up ending the betrothal.

"Why don't you ever speak of your time away?" She plucked at the fabric of her gown, her gaze holding on it rather than him.

A denial was on the tip of his tongue. But she was right. "Much of it was inconsequential. Boring, if you will."

"Not all of it."

"No." He stared across the garden but didn't see the bright blooms or shrubbery. Instead, he saw the rugged terrain of New Zealand covered with soldiers.

The wars there had started as small skirmishes over land disputes but quickly escalated when the Māori, the Polynesian people native to New Zealand, protested the colonial government and their land sales. The worst of the wars had seen 18,000 British troops, along with artillery and cavalry, involved in heavy fighting in dense bush.

While the British military had far outnumbered the Māori and their supporters and had superior weaponry, the battles were intense. The Māori's war tactics using bunkers and fortified villages had surprised the British with their effectiveness. The warriors had been highly maneuverable and inflicted heavy losses on the British.

Michael had been torn during his time there as to which side was right. Of course, his allegiance was to the British Army to whom he'd pledged an oath. But his sympathies were often with the Māori. The government had confiscated their land as punishment for the uprisings but that seemed unfair to Michael and had angered the Māori even more.

The escalating situation had dimmed his desire to serve his country.

However, sharing any of those details with family and friends felt disloyal to England. Who was he to declare that colonization of far-flung countries should be questioned? Were the circumstances of the people living in those areas improved after British interference? The answer depended on who was asked.

Leaving the army seemed the best solution, and he still believed that to be true. However, the restlessness he'd experienced upon returning home had been unexpected. The sleepless nights less so. Though he had to admit that since he and Tibby had become betrothed, both of those had eased.

On the nights he found himself wide awake, he'd been able to clear his mind of bad memories by working on the mystery. That was much more effective than tossing and turning. Tibby's suggestion of him writing a book had been a gift in more than one way.

He glanced at her, debating on what, if anything, to say.

"My time in New Zealand proved difficult in numerous ways. The thick bush made fighting a challenge. But the reason we were fighting left a sour taste in my mouth."

Rather than ask questions or respond with platitudes, Tibby simply waited to see if he'd say more.

He looked away, preferring not to see if her expression turned to one of disapproval. "I wasn't in complete agreement with senior officers as to how the situation was managed. The Māori, the people native to the area, had a right to the land. Certainly more than the British."

"I can't imagine how conflicted that must've left you. I read some of the accounts in the news sheet about the situation."

"You did?" Few ladies of his acquaintance bothered with reading news, especially when it involved war.

"From what your mother had told me, I knew you were there." She glanced at her clasped hands, a hint of color rising in her cheeks. Then she lifted her gaze to meet his. "I wanted to better understand what you might be experiencing."

His mouth went dry at the realization that she'd been thinking of him to that extent. While he had thought of her off and on over the years, he wouldn't have guessed that he was on her mind often enough for her to be interested in where he was or what he was doing.

"I should have written you more often," he said. Tibby had sent letters on a regular basis. But as the years passed, he'd rarely bothered to respond. It had come as no surprise when she'd written him less and less.

"I enjoyed the ones you sent. They were entertaining *and* interesting, which is why I thought you should consider writing a book. Your observations were fascinating. But I'm sure you became busier as your career advanced."

How like her to make excuses for him. "In truth, more often it was because I didn't have anything good to say."

She smiled, but it didn't reach her eyes. "Nor did I after a time."

He ached at the realization of how her world had been narrowing with each year that passed. He'd never considered that. In fact, he'd pictured her moving on with her life and enjoying the events and opportunities that had filled his time before he'd left England.

"Enough of such dreary subjects," he declared with a wave of his hand. He preferred a genuine smile on her face, one that brightened her eyes with joy. He hadn't invited her to this picnic to make her sad. "Tell me of the book club to which you belong."

"The Mayfair Literary League is comprised of six of us, including me, at the moment. But our membership might be expanding."

"What kind of books do you read?" he asked as the footman returned with a selection of desserts that he left on the table before departing.

"All types. We've read several Jane Austen stories, of course. But we also read books that touch on current issues that face us all. Ones that bring to light the terrible conditions in the poorer areas of London. I highly recommend *The Seven Curses of London* if you're interested in such things. The stories in it moved our members so much that we added a charity component to our league."

"How interesting." Michael could easily imagine Tibby being outraged enough by injustices to take action. "What else?"

"Mysteries, of course," she said with a pointed look at him. "I can only imagine the other members' delight if I happened to know the author of one."

He laughed. "That won't come to pass for some time, if at all."

"We shall see. I know how determined you become when you set your mind to something."

"Hmm." She really did know him well. Yet she was so different than the Tibby he remembered—deeper and more complex. And certainly more beautiful with her long-limbed grace and those brown eyes that watched him with interest.

They spoke of inconsequential things for a time, enjoying one of the apple tarts along with a small, iced cake.

"Delicious," Tibby declared as she licked icing from a finger.

Desire speared through Michael, the intensity of it catching his breath. She looked especially beautiful today. Perhaps it was because she'd appeared so frail and tired the last time he'd seen her.

Her gown was a pale lavender with white flowers embroidered on the overskirt. Her hair was loosely bound, making her look especially feminine and appealing.

Damn, but he needed another kiss. Immediately if not sooner.

He shifted closer and braced himself on one elbow, lifting his other hand to touch her bare arm.

Her gaze flew to his, awareness in the depth of her eyes. She looked almost startled by his touch.

That seemed fair because the way she made him feel startled him. He dearly wanted to know if her body stirred the way his did when she was near.

"Tibby?" he whispered, his focus shifting to her delicate pink lips, wondering how sweet they might taste.

"Yes?" Her breath was coming quicker, her chest rising and falling as if her heart raced.

He lifted her hand and placed it over his own heart, hoping she could feel its quick beat. "I would like to kiss you again."

"Oh." She blinked several times. "I mean yes. I would like that, too."

Her eyes darkened, whether from need or excitement, he didn't know. He remained where he was, hoping she'd initiate the kiss.

That only lasted a moment. Until the confusion crossing her face had him reaching for her. What had he expected when she was clearly so innocent?

He cupped the back of her head and drew her forward. When she was no more than an inch away, he lightened his hold, hoping—needing—her to come the rest of the way.

She hesitated, clearly out of her element. Then she released a breath and leaned forward to press her lips to his.

Victory had never tasted so sweet. Certainly, it might have been because of the cake she'd just eaten. But it was more than that.

Her kissing him was an admission of sorts that said she wanted him. That he was more to her than a convenient friend willing to aid her.

With each day that passed, he hoped even more that it was true. His tenderness for her was special. His need for her was overwhelming at times. Who knew where those feelings might lead?

He deepened the kiss, pressing his tongue along the seam of her lips until she parted for him, allowing him entrance. Another sweet victory.

As if she were enjoying their intimacy as much as he was, she moved the hand that rested on his chest, slipping it inside his jacket. That small invasion sent his pulse hammering. Her tongue moved alongside his, slowly at first. Then quicker as if she were anxious to experience more.

With a low growl, he pulled her against him and devoured. He knew it was too much too soon. After all, they weren't truly betrothed. But he couldn't help himself.

To his shock, Tibby gave as good as she got. She kissed his cheek, his jaw, then moved back to his mouth in a deep kiss, while her hand caressed his chest and caused his body to stir with desire.

The passion that flooded him so quickly was shocking. To think this was Tibby in his arms made it even more so. He reached for her breast, silently cursing the clothing between them. Tibby arched into his hand with a low moan, clearly enjoying the moment, too.

Suddenly she stiffened and jerked back to stare at him, eyes glazed with desire but wide with alarm.

He couldn't begin to guess what she might be thinking. Somehow, he had the feeling it wasn't good.

With a gasp, she clambered to her feet, chest heaving as she smoothed her skirts. "I—" She shook her head and was gone before he could protest.

Chapter Thirteen

B y the next morning, Tibby had yet to come to terms with what had happened at the picnic and her part in those heated moments, not to mention her abrupt departure.

What must Michael think of her? That she was a wanton, lonely woman so desperate for attention that she kissed her best friend every chance she could get?

Oh, dear heaven.

She sank onto her bed and rubbed both hands over her cheeks. She'd had a clear intent when she'd joined Michael in the garden—to end their betrothal. After considering the matter at length, she had thought it best to break it off now.

The plan had become too complicated. Their pretend relationship was hurting others, most notably, her mother.

But even more, Tibby worried that she was losing her heart to Michael. There would be nothing left of her when he walked away. And she couldn't allow herself to believe he wouldn't, despite her hopes or her plan.

She wasn't the sort of woman with whom men fell in love. That had become clear after meeting many over the course of the last six years during which she'd attended balls and events. No one in particular had expressed interest in her.

The few men who'd been a part of her life had easily walked away when the need arose. How sad was it that she had the same fear as her mother? That she'd be alone for the rest of her life.

Michael's thoughtfulness would be the death of her. The picnic had been so sweet, a delightful port of call in the rocky seas of her life. But it didn't mean he was falling in love with her, and she wasn't sure she could settle for anything less.

The question was, what did she do now? Did she break the betrothal before Michael had a chance to suggest she do so? Did she hold out for a few more weeks and hope he eventually came to see her as something more than a friend?

Their heated kiss suggested it was possible. Then again, men and women kissed all the time without it meaning anything significant. She'd witnessed enough of that on darkened terraces and hidden corners of ballrooms over the years.

She was no young debutante and should know better than to set her sights so high. But considering how long she'd ached for Michael to think of her as more than a friend, was it any wonder that she wanted more than a renewed friendship with him?

If someone had seen them in the garden, their betrothal would no longer be pretend. They needed to take care, lest they be forced to marry sooner rather than later, and the option to break off the betrothal would be gone.

Though she would welcome marrying him as she'd dreamed of a life with him for some time, never did she want him to be forced into it.

Now she better understood how Phoebe must have felt when she and the Earl of Bolton had been caught in a compromising situation. Though Phoebe had cared for Bolton for a long while, she hadn't wanted them to be forced to marry either.

Tibby rose once again to pace the length of her room, her thoughts swirling as she considered what to do.

A knock on the door had her turning to face it, worry filling her that her mother had taken a turn for the worse. "Yes?"

"Good morning, Tibby." Aunt Eleanor opened the door, her perpetual smile in place. "I wanted to see what your plans were for the day."

As always, her aunt's dark hair was drawn back into a knot at the base of her neck, and she looked vaguely like her older sister. But kind brown eyes set in a round face and a plump figure made her different. She was a sturdy soul, both in spirit and appearance.

Her presence had been a welcome relief after Tibby's bedside vigil and worry over the past week. She was much different than her older sister in manner if not looks. She'd married young and had raised two daughters, both of whom were starting families of their own.

Aunt Eleanor was warm-hearted, efficient, and level-headed. She listened to her sister's numerous complaints then countered them with a positive view. She was soft-spoken but firm and tended to see the bright side of life.

Tibby's father had often remarked on how much Tibby was like her. In the past few years, Tibby had wished her own mother was more like Aunt Eleanor though she'd never admit it to her mother.

"I don't have anything specific planned. Is there something you need?"

"Not at all. However, I wondered when I would have the chance to meet your Captain Shaw."

My Captain Shaw. If only he truly was hers. If only she wasn't lying to everyone.

Tibby dearly wanted to talk to someone about the situation since it seemed to be growing more complicated with each day that passed, but it couldn't be her aunt. Phoebe was the ideal person but was still gone. Perhaps she could call on Harriet to ask her opinion on how to proceed.

The next literary league meeting was next week. Tibby would be expected to share her progress but had yet to decide what to say.

Her aunt lifted a brow, clearly waiting for an answer to what should be a simple question.

If only it was.

"I'm sure he will come by in the next day or two." Would he? Given the fact that she'd left the picnic he'd arranged so abruptly, it seemed unlikely.

"Why don't you invite him for tea this afternoon?"

Nerves tightened her stomach at the idea of facing his questioning looks. He'd want an explanation for her behavior. "I thought perhaps we should wait until Mother is feeling better before we have visitors."

"Nonsense." Aunt Eleanor smiled. "I can't think of a more effective way to hurry along her recovery than for her to know she's missing out on something."

Tibby sighed. "I'm not certain that would matter. The last few times I attended a ball without her, she made her displeasure clear. But she still refused my suggestion for her to join me if I went to another."

"We'll see if we can change her thoughts on staying home so often. It's not good for her." Aunt Eleanor shook her head. "I thought I had her convinced to go out more during my last visit. I'm sorry to hear she hasn't changed." She stepped farther inside the room and closed the door. "How did she take the news of your betrothal?"

"Not well." Tibby pressed her fingertips to her chest as an ache stirred there. She still worried that the news had contributed to her illness.

"I'm sorry for that." Aunt Eleanor walked forward and took Tibby's hands in her own. "Don't let it sway you. She will be fine after you marry."

"I don't know that she will. It's been seven years since Father passed. If anything, she's gotten worse." It was a relief to speak to someone about her worry on this topic, at least. Victor only grew angry at their mother when Tibby broached the subject.

"I wish I better understood her," Aunt Eleanor said, releasing Tibby's hands. "If she wants you to stay, why wouldn't she do more to ensure your happiness?"

"Using guilt is more effective." Tibby squeezed her eyes shut at the admission, already wishing she hadn't said it.

"Of course, you're right." Aunt Eleanor moved to Tibby's window to stare out. "The situation is more complicated than I realized."

Tibby heaved another sigh. "I shouldn't have said that. I love Mother dearly. It's just—"

"You want a future of your own." She turned to look at Tibby. "A family of your own."

Longing pierced through her at those words. Although she'd made a daring move with Michael, she didn't believe he'd suddenly fall in love with her. She had realized years ago that the chances of marrying were nil. Therefore, the possibility of ever holding her child was as well.

In truth, she couldn't imagine any version of that future without Michael at her side. How silly of her to pin her hopes on their pretend betrothal. He'd only just returned after being gone a decade and had his own future to plan.

Her secret wish had to remain just that—a secret.

However, like everyone else, her aunt believed the betrothal was real. Perhaps she should share her doubt so it wouldn't come as much of a surprise when it ended.

"Yes, but..." Tibby hesitated, searching for a way to hint that she had doubts without casting blame on Michael. "I suppose I worry that Michael hasn't yet had a chance to adjust to life at home. He's been gone for most of the past decade."

"I'm sure his return will require an adjustment. Life in the army couldn't have been easy."

Tibby's heart squeezed as she considered what he'd shared the previous day. She was touched he'd told her as much as he had. What a difficult position he'd been in. "We should've waited a year or two until he'd adapted to life at home again."

"Are you worried you were able to snatch him up before he could meet someone else?" Aunt Eleanor asked with a smile.

"Yes, I am. There are many lovely young ladies who would make fine wives." Better than she would. Ones who didn't have a demanding mother. "The fact that we've been friends since childhood gave me an unfair advantage."

"Oh, Tibby. You don't think he proposed simply because you're a comfortable option, do you?"

He hadn't proposed. But she couldn't admit that. "I'm more like an old pair of boots. Much preferable to the new ones that pinch your toes."

"I refuse to allow you to say such things. You're a lovely person inside and out. He'd be a fool not to see that for himself. I'm sure you're much different than the friend he left behind."

Was she? While he'd seen and done many things in those ten years, she hadn't ventured any farther than Bath to see her aunt and cousins. She had many of the same friends. Her days followed the same pattern as before. No wonder she loved to read to expand her narrow life.

None of that provided her with experiences comparable to his. However, Michael *had* changed, and she feared she had little to offer him.

How could he possibly ever come to love her?

"Tibby, if you have concerns, you should share them with your Captain Shaw. I'm sure he'll help you see things differently." She smiled with a confidence that Tibby was far from feeling. "Now then, what you've told me settles it. Invite him for tea this afternoon, and I'll be sure to give you a few minutes alone so the two of you can have a heart-to-heart conversation. Some of Society's rules are ridiculous. A couple prepared to marry should be allowed time alone together. How else can you come to know each other better?"

Aunt Eleanor had thought Tibby had joined Michael and his mother and grandmother yesterday for the picnic, and Tibby hadn't bothered to correct her. While Tibby agreed with her aunt's opinion about rules for proper behavior, time alone with Michael wouldn't solve anything. It would only complicate it further.

Her aunt patted her on the shoulder as she moved past her toward the door. "Let me know if he's available. I look forward to meeting him."

WOULD YOU LIKE TO COME to tea? Aunt Eleanor wants to meet you.

T

Michael studied the message, trying to guess what Tibby might be thinking. He was still stunned and hurt at the way she'd bolted yesterday.

While he'd thought they were in agreement about their relationship, that clearly wasn't the case. Then again, what did he expect when he had yet to define what it was?

He certainly hadn't made any sort of declaration as to how he felt but hoped his actions spoke for him. Was he ready to say more?

His mind balked at the thought. He needed more time. Time to adjust to the change in his life. To determine a career path. While he had funds from selling his commission and a small inheritance his father had left him, those wouldn't provide enough in the coming years. Especially not if he married.

In truth, he'd been rather certain he wouldn't take a wife. The idea of having someone underfoot all the time had been less than appealing. Yet he couldn't deny that sharing his days with Tibby was a joy. Whether it was memories or the results of his botany experiments or ideas for the mystery, she was an excellent listener. She'd contribute to whatever plan he decided to pursue and would share her opinions along the way.

She would never be in his way. He felt more at peace when she was with him. The fact that he was becoming addicted to their kisses was another reason to start thinking about the future. He was more than ready to move forward on the physical side of their relationship.

Did his feelings amount to love?

He didn't know. He'd never been in love before. Certainly, he'd experienced his share of lust. That alone convinced him there was more to his feelings for Tibby than anything he'd previously experienced.

If only their alliance hadn't shifted to a pretend betrothal. Then he could consider courting her and move forward—or not—from there. Instead, the need to pretend they were further along in their relationship than they were weighed on them both, coloring their feelings.

Had she been pretending yesterday? Surely not. He would've known. At least, he hoped so. Besides, there hadn't been a reason to since they'd been alone.

He pressed a hand to his temple, unsurprised at the ache developing there. What a tangled knot the situation had become.

"Is something amiss, Michael?" His grandmother entered the drawing room where he stood with the message in hand.

"Not at all." He forced a smile and lifted the note. "I've been invited to tea with Lady Tabitha and her aunt this afternoon."

"That must mean Lady Dunford is feeling better."

"Yes, she's on the mend. Whether she'll be joining us for tea remains to be seen. I don't believe she's pleased with my betrothal to Tibby."

His grandmother settled in her favorite chair and reached for her needlework. "Don't take it personally. I don't think she'd approve of anyone who might take away her daughter."

"Perhaps, but her opinion makes the situation difficult for Tibby."

"All the more reason she has you for support. I like Tabitha. The girl has a fine mind, something that seems to be missing among the latest crop of debutantes."

"True," Michael agreed. He'd overheard a conversation or two at the few events he attended and could only shake his head at the inane topics discussed by some ladies.

"If the younger generation bothered to read a book or two, they'd be better for it," his grandmother continued as she took practiced stitches with a bright red thread.

"Tabitha belongs to a literary league. From what she said, they read a wide variety of books."

"All the more reason to admire her. I'm pleased the two of you have found a deeper connection."

He hoped that was true. After sending a reply that he'd be pleased to join them for tea, he went to the greenhouse to check on his experiments, something he'd failed to do of late. Very little had changed but at least the ones he'd grafted were still attached.

Then he returned to the desk in his room to look over the notes on his book. He paused to run a hand over Tibby's gloves which sat on the edge of his desk as he had yet to return them. Perhaps he truly was becoming smitten. If that was true, he needed to determine his own future first, especially the financial aspect of it. Supporting himself was simple enough but supporting a family was much different.

More than ready to set aside his churning thoughts, he turned his attention to his notes. The pleasure of crafting a mystery continued to surprise him. He'd already created a clever, if inexperienced, protagonist and an evil villain with a motive for murder.

After a brief break for luncheon, he returned to his list of potential suspects but kept a careful eye on the clock so he wouldn't be late for tea.

Tea with Tibby. That brought him even more pleasure than the mystery. What did that say about his feelings for her?

He knocked on the door at Dunford House promptly at four o'clock and was shown into the drawing room where Tibby and her aunt awaited him.

He studied Tibby and though she briefly met his gaze, he didn't see any of the panic that had been so clearly written on her face when she'd left the previous day.

He wanted a moment alone with her to make certain he hadn't offended her with his advances. After all, this was supposed to be a *pretend* betrothal. Yet he couldn't seem to remember that when they were together.

"It's a pleasure to meet you, Captain," Tibby's aunt said with a warm smile after Tibby introduced him. "I've heard many good things about you."

Mrs. Cameron was a friendlier, rounder version of her sister with dark hair and a forthright manner. Her gown was simple but in good taste, her lively brown eyes suggesting she found much to enjoy in life.

"I've heard the same of you, Mrs. Cameron." He glanced at Tibby then took a seat. "I'm so pleased you were able to come for a visit right when you were needed."

"I was planning to visit soon anyway. Victor's message prompted me to do so earlier. How nice that you live next door."

"Indeed." He nodded. "Quite convenient." The pointed look Tibby shared with her aunt left him guessing at its meaning. "I'm lucky to have known Lady Tabitha and her family for years."

"I met your mother and grandmother a few years ago during one of my previous visits. Please give them my regards."

"I will be certain to. How is Lady Dunford faring?"

"Regaining her strength," Tibby said as she served tea. "She has been up and about, walking in her room the past two days, thanks to Aunt Eleanor's insistence."

"It's always better to keep the body moving in my experience. Don't you agree, Captain?"

"I certainly prefer a more active lifestyle."

"As does our Tabitha." Mrs. Cameron smiled at her niece. "From what she's told me, you enjoy gardening almost as much as she does."

"Any excuse to be outside is welcome. I have been trying my hand at creating a new variety of roses, but it's too soon to say whether it will be a success."

The conversation continued with Mrs. Cameron guiding it. Michael felt as if he were being interviewed and hoped for Tibby's sake that he provided the right answers.

It seemed to take some time before Tibby began to relax. Again, he wondered what was bothering her and whether it had anything to do with yesterday.

"It's been a pleasure meeting you," Mrs. Cameron said after they'd finished tea. "I'll leave the two of you to enjoy a little time together while I check on my sister."

Michael stood when she did. "The pleasure was mine. I look forward to visiting with you again soon." He rather wished she were Tibby's mother, though he certainly wouldn't tell anyone that.

The moment she stepped out of the room, he turned to Tibby, hesitating whether to approach her. "Is all well?"

Tibby slowly met his gaze. "Please accept my apologies for my poor behavior yesterday." She slowly stood, keeping her voice low.

"I'm the one who should apologize. I didn't mean to upset you." He walked closer until they were no more than a hand's width apart. Still, it seemed too far.

"You didn't." Her hand fluttered in the air before she allowed it to fall. "The...situation is overwhelming at times."

If only he knew what she meant. "Do you refer to our betrothal?"

She nodded. "We've discussed this before but pretending is more difficult than I expected."

Pretending you care for me? He couldn't bring himself to ask when he wasn't certain of the answer. Of course, she cared for him. But in what way?

"Aunt Eleanor thinks my mother will adjust to the betrothal, but I remain unconvinced."

He nodded, wishing her mother's state of mind—and health—wasn't a concern. "Given that she wasn't happy before we announced our betrothal, I think we need to give it more time. Isn't it too soon to know whether it will work? Now that your aunt is here, perhaps she can help persuade your mother to make some changes given the circumstances."

"Perhaps," Tibby said, though her pensive expression suggested she wasn't convinced. "I suppose another week or two won't matter given that our plan is already underway. We will know more then."

"Yes," he readily agreed. "We both will." Additional time would allow his confusion to clear. If his feelings for her were growing deeper than friendship, he had some planning to do.

Chapter Fourteen

"What a lovely day for a ride." Tibby reached down to pat her mare's dappled grey neck. She released a breath, pleased to also release her poor mood. Michael's parting words the previous day had confused her and caused a sleepless night.

"I'm pleased you could join me," Michael said with a smile. "Is the mare to your liking?"

"Oh, yes." He'd been kind enough to offer her one of their horses since she and her mother didn't have any appropriate for a jaunt like this. "I haven't ridden for an age. I've missed it more than I thought."

"I had more than my share of being on horseback while in the army, but I still enjoy it."

Michael led the way down the street toward Hyde Park. The air was warm but not overly so. Scattered clouds kept the temperature moderate.

When he'd invited her to ride in Hyde Park before her mother had fallen ill, she assumed he'd meant in a carriage. This was even better.

Her heart had lifted at the unexpected excursion he'd suggested only an hour earlier. However, the invitation had only added to her confusion. His remark the previous day stating they would *both* know more if they gave their betrothal more time made no sense. He'd seemed almost relieved at her agreement to continue it. What did that mean?

Riding horses was something she'd done frequently in her youth, especially during their months in the country, often with Michael. But after her father had passed away, Victor sold some of the horses. Once he'd married, she and her mother rarely joined them in the country, not wanting to intrude on the newly wedded couple.

Tibby's gaze lingered on the military bearing of the man who rode just ahead of her, admiring his broad shoulders in the brown jacket and the narrow hips that moved easily with his gelding.

Her riding habit was sadly out of date. She hadn't bothered to order any new ones since she no longer rode. She ran a gloved hand along the navy blue fabric, hoping her appearance wasn't an embarrassment to him.

He cast a glance over his shoulder, his grin catching her breath. At that moment, she realized how good he'd been for her. If nothing else, the past month had given her the gift of his friendship again. She needed to do everything in her power to make certain she didn't lose that when they parted ways.

Refusing to allow dark thoughts of a bleak future to ruin her mood, she shoved them aside and kneed her horse to catch up to Michael so they might enter the park together.

"I've forgotten how well you ride," Michael said, admiration in his eyes as his gaze swept over her.

The compliment created a warm bubble of pleasure deep inside her. "Thank you. I've forgotten how much I enjoy it."

"Then we'll plan on doing more of it."

The suggestion that involved the future threatened to pop the bubble, but she pushed back the threat as they rode side by side along the path. The park was busy and several times they paused to allow a vehicle to pass.

At last, they reached the open meadow.

"Care for a race?" she asked Michael.

His eyes lit with her challenge. Before he could agree, she kneed her horse and loosened the reins, encouraging the mare to gallop.

The horse raced forward, seeming to thoroughly enjoy the freedom to run. Tibby glanced over her shoulder to see Michael in hot pursuit. A laugh escaped, turning the heads of several other riders. Tibby didn't care. Let them stare.

He soon caught up to her, taking the lead once or twice before she pushed her steed a little more. His laugh caused her to do the same as he pulled back.

She slowed her horse as well, straightening her hat which had come loose in her flight across the field.

"You always were able to beat me," Michael said as he rode alongside her.

"Only because you let me," she countered.

"You are a fierce competitor. That's one of the many things I've always admired about you."

A competitor? She supposed she had been. But that quality had faded in the last few years. Now she considered herself more of a survivor.

"I've missed you so, Michael." The words slipped out unbidden when she'd only meant to think them. She pressed her lips tight, not wanting him to think she'd been pining for him the entire time he'd been gone.

"I missed you, too, Tibby. Only in the past weeks have I recognized how much."

Her stomach fluttered at the warmth in his expression even as desire stirred deep within her. She wanted more than a few heated kisses with this man. But doing so would risk her heart.

Would it be worth it?

If forced to decide at this moment, she would've said yes. The realization was terrifying.

By silent agreement, they continued on, talking little as they made their way toward the river. The view was wonderful, bringing to mind the countryside. She'd been in Hyde Park more times than she could count but never failed to be amazed that this piece of what felt like the countryside sat in the middle of London.

"How's your mother today?" Michael asked at length.

"Continuing to improve. Aunt Eleanor was going to take her out to the garden to sit for a time while I was gone. She said the fresh air would do her good."

"I like your aunt. She and your mother are quite different."

"It's amazing to think they were raised in the same household by the same parents, isn't it?" Tibby pondered the matter further. "Though I tend to think they were more alike in their younger days. Certainly, before Father died."

"I'm sorry how deeply his death affected her. She must've really loved him."

"She did. But I think she allowed her life to revolve around his too much. Most wives do, of course. She did so at the cost of her own. I didn't see that until he was gone." She stared at the river, noting the currents taking leaves and sticks along in its wake. Much like life did with people. Perhaps her mother needed a new current of sorts to push her along. "I wonder if it would be possible for her to love again."

"Take another husband?" Michael asked, his tone one of surprise.

"Not that anyone could replace Father. But..." She shrugged. "Silly to suggest it, I suppose."

"Maybe not. I hate to think of my mother alone when my grandmother passes on. Though having a relationship while your husband's mother lives with you could be complicated."

Tibby laughed. "Very true. Maybe I'll mention the idea to Aunt Eleanor to see what she thinks. It wouldn't hurt to introduce Mother to a few gentlemen her age. That is if I'm able to persuade her to leave the house."

"I hope her illness has made her appreciate life more. Perhaps that will provide the impetus for being more social."

"One can hope," Tibby said with a sigh.

"Would you care to walk for a bit?" he asked.

"Excellent idea."

He guided them toward a grove of trees then helped her to dismount. Was it her imagination or did his hands linger on her waist after he'd lifted her down?

She couldn't bring herself to look at him too closely. Not when she was already struggling to keep the moment light. She didn't want him to see the longing that must be visible in her eyes. He took their reins and tied them to a low branch, leaving the horses to graze.

He offered his arm, and she was pleased when he pressed it tight against him as they strolled along.

She'd expected him to follow the path along the river. Instead, he meandered into the trees.

"It's lovely here," she whispered as she studied the tall oaks that surrounded them, giving a small measure of privacy.

He paused and turned to face her. "Almost as lovely as you."

Her breath caught at the sweet compliment. She shouldn't read too much into his remark. But it struck one more gaping hole in the meager defenses that protected her heart. She glanced away, uncertain how to respond.

"Tabitha, you truly are beautiful."

Her attention was fully caught by his use of her formal name. It made her feel like someone else. Someone better. Someone worthy of this handsome captain. "Thank you. How kind of you to say so."

"Why is it that I think you don't hear it nearly enough?" He took her gloved hand and held it between both of his bare ones.

She laughed, embarrassed. "Somehow our pretend betrothal has colored your view." It was the only explanation. She wasn't beautiful. Far from it. Yet she wouldn't deny that she'd always dreamed of meeting a man who thought her so.

"I saw it before our betrothal started."

Her heart hammered at his admission. It hammered even harder at his failure to add the word 'pretend.' Didn't he understand that she needed to be reminded that this wasn't real? "You mean our *pretend* betrothal."

"However you prefer to describe it." His gaze dropped to her lips, and he leaned close to capture her mouth with his.

Tibby stiffened in surprise but only for a moment. Then she gave in to the kiss, leaning against him as close as she dared. His arms reached to hold her tight.

One thing she knew for certain. She wasn't going to run this time. She intended to take as much as Michael offered and enjoy every moment.

Tibby reached up to wrap her hands around his shoulders, wishing she didn't have on gloves. Taking them off would take too long. The thin leather didn't stop her from running her fingers along his hair and neck.

She loved the way he held her as if she were a treasured object that he adored and couldn't get enough of. No wonder she thought so often about his kisses and what might follow.

He pulled back to kiss her jaw and down her neck. The high neckline of the riding habit didn't allow him to go far. He squeezed her waist before running his hands over her hips, making her body ache.

The feelings coursing through her were unfamiliar yet thrilling.

"Tibby," Michael muttered. "You're driving me mad."

She frowned, confused as to how that could be when she wasn't doing anything. Should she apologize?

"I—" The sound of voices cut off whatever he'd been about to say.

He stepped away and turned to the side, cursing under his breath.

A group of people was approaching. Tibby knew they couldn't risk being caught alone like this. It would cause expectations that they set a date for a wedding they never intended to have. Her thoughts scattered.

Luckily, Michael took her elbow and strode toward where they'd left the horses at a rather hurried pace. His steps were so quick that she had to skip to keep up with him. Obviously, he didn't want to be caught either.

The thought was a sobering one.

They returned to the horses without being seen. Tibby was disappointed when Michael made no effort to complete what he'd been about to tell her before that.

Then again, maybe it was for the best. If he'd intended to apologize for those kisses, she didn't want to hear it. Not when she dearly hoped they would be able to repeat the experience soon.

She'd worry about her heart later, after they'd parted ways.

"CAPTAIN SHAW."

Michael reached out to shake Major Winters' hand, though the temptation to salute him nearly overtook the handshake. "Good to see you, Major."

Winters' message for them to meet had come as a surprise. Michael had found it waiting for him after returning from his ride with Tibby the previous day. At the very least, it was a welcome distraction from the unfamiliar emotions spiraling through him.

If those people hadn't interrupted them in Hyde Park, what might he have said? Was his desire for Tibby overruling his good sense? Did he truly have feelings for her or was this lust? He thought he knew the difference but couldn't seem to properly identify what he felt.

His confusion had kept him from saying much of anything as they returned home. They'd parted with vague promises to talk again soon.

His life was far from settled. He'd only just returned home. How could he possibly think of a long-term commitment with anyone when he didn't know where he'd be living or what he'd be doing two months from now? He might have enough funds to support himself for a time if he lived modestly, but not to properly care for a wife.

Mind-numbing kisses shouldn't sway him from his plan to wait to see where their relationship led. Thank goodness she'd had on a riding habit, or he might've taken their intimacy much further.

Michael pulled his thoughts back to Major Winters as they both sat at a secluded table in the Naval and Military Club on St. James's Square.

"I didn't realize you were in London," Michael said.

While not his commanding officer, Michael knew the older man fairly well. They'd both spent several years in New Zealand and had shared a few of their concerns over a bottle of whisky or two on numerous occasions.

"I retired soon after you did. I decided I'd had enough of living abroad. My wife agreed," Winters added with a smile. His erect bearing and neatly trimmed salt-and-pepper hair and sideburns marked him as a military man.

"How are you finding London?" Michael asked, curious as the major had always been a man of action. If Michael was finding the adjustment to civilian life difficult, Winters must find it doubly so.

Winters held his gaze for a long moment. "Not as appealing as I expected in all honesty."

"Oh?"

"The days are surprisingly long without duties to fill them."

"I have found the same." Michael was relieved to learn he wasn't the only one with those thoughts. "It will take time to become accustomed to it, I suppose."

"I'm not given to idleness. My wife continually tells me to relax, but it's not that easy. A lack of purpose makes me restless. Have you discovered something to fill your days?" Winters asked.

"Botany was my first choice."

"Botany." Winters' brow furrowed. "Growing roses, are you?"

Michael pursed his lips. It sounded terribly boring put like that. "Something of the sort." He didn't care to explain further. Especially when he wasn't really enjoying it. "However, I've since moved on to a new pastime."

The satisfaction that took hold as his thoughts turned to writing the mystery novel surprised him. Yet the hobby was too new to share with anyone other than Tibby. Did he feel comfortable speaking with her about it because she'd suggested it, because she was a good friend, or something else?

That was another question he couldn't yet answer.

Winters leaned forward, elbows on the table. "I ran into an old friend, a member of the nobility, who needs assistance. I'm hoping this task might lead to similar ones. I could think of no one I'd rather have to join me than you."

"Oh?" Michael was intrigued.

"I need something to do, or my wife tells me she'll find something for me." Winters chuckled. "That is never a good thing."

"I don't suppose." Michael smiled. He'd met Mrs. Winters on numerous occasions and wouldn't want to have the intimidating woman cross with him.

"My friend needs to transfer some valuable documents and has asked for a secure escort. He would pay handsomely if the mission were successful."

"How far do they need to go?"

"From London to Manchester."

"That's a significant distance."

"I don't know if a security detail is something you're interested in doing long term, but if your schedule permits you to assist me this time, I would consider it a personal favor."

"Are you certain you want me to accompany you?"

"I have no doubt. You're one of the most dependable, discreet, and honest men I've had the pleasure of knowing. We'll need at least two additional men as well."

Winters named the fee, tempting Michael further. Having more funds in the bank would be welcome, no matter what his future held.

"Very well. I'll join you."

"Excellent." Winters clapped him on the shoulder.

They discussed possible routes and the length of the journey, as well as the dangers and the need for secrecy. Michael couldn't deny the challenge brought a certain excitement. Whether he wanted to do this again remained to be seen.

One thing he knew for certain was that his mother and grandmother wouldn't like it.

"As I mentioned, secrecy is of the utmost importance," Winters continued. "No one can know our true purpose or the final destination. My friend insists on it as he fears if certain individuals learn the documents are being moved, they'll try to take them."

Michael wanted to know what they were but didn't bother to ask. "How soon do you want to leave?"

"In the next few days, if possible. But first, we need to see who could join us, as well as the rest of our plans."

Perhaps a few days away from London would be good, Michael thought. Some distance from Tibby and the complicated feelings she brought forth might provide clarity. He hoped so at any rate.

Winters rose from the table and shook Michael's hand. "I couldn't be more pleased that you've agreed to accompany me. This could prove lucrative if all goes well."

"Always good to have funds for the future."

"That sounds as if you've been giving the future some thought." Winters lifted a brow. "Does that mean you have specific plans? Marriage perhaps?"

It was on the tip of his tongue to say that he was betrothed. But how could he claim that when Tibby continued to remind him it was only pretend? Granted, he hadn't given her any reason to believe otherwise.

"Nothing is firmly set," he said, wondering when—or if—he'd be prepared to change that.

"It sounds as if I caught you at the right time then. Plan on meeting here again tomorrow afternoon. We'll finalize the details then."

Chapter Fifteen

"May I ask a question, Aunt Eleanor?" Tibby looked up from her embroidery to study her aunt.

They had been sitting together in the drawing room, working on their needlework in what had been companionable silence.

Tibby had given much thought to what she mentioned to Michael about her mother. What if she could find a gentleman who caught her mother's eye? The lure of friends hadn't been enough to convince her to leave the house on a regular basis. Did that mean a gentleman wouldn't either?

Perhaps the idea was silly. Yet she couldn't put it from her mind. At this point, it seemed like it was worth a try. Never mind that she had no idea how to go about finding a man in whom her mother might be interested.

"Of course, dear." Her aunt looked at her expectantly. "What is it?"

"Do you think it would be possible for Mother to marry again?"

Aunt Eleanor paused in surprise, her hands stilling on her needlepoint. "Is there someone she's been seeing?"

"Not at all." Tibby shook her head. "It's probably ridiculous for me to even raise the question. I just thought that meeting a

185

gentleman might be a way to change her thinking and give her some joy in life."

"I'm sure you're right. Though I don't know how we could convince her of that. She loved your father deeply. She might feel as if she were betraying him if she so much as looked at another man."

"That is my concern as well. But still, I wonder if it's worth a try. All I know is that she's unhappy. I don't like seeing her like this. I want her to find contentment, at least."

"As do I." Aunt Eleanor smiled. "I suppose the fact that you have become betrothed brought you the idea. Those in love always want the same for the people around them."

Tibby's cheeks heated. It was on the tip of her tongue to deny her aunt's words. But she couldn't when it was becoming true.

She had always cared for Michael, and the more time she spent with him, the deeper her feelings grew. While his recent displays of affection made her hope that he was beginning to see her as more than a friend, he hadn't *said* anything to confirm that.

She couldn't make him fall in love with her. Certainly, she'd hoped that planting the idea might cause it to bloom, but she also worried that if it didn't, she would lose him as a friend. That would be a terrible result of her bold move.

She walked a fine line—a tight rope, much like a circus performer, taking one step at a time across a high wire. The stakes were great, and she had no idea if she would succeed. Nor had she anticipated how complicated the situation would be.

Tibby didn't like deceiving her family and friends. She hadn't even liked sharing her betrothal with Lady Lucinda and Lady Jane, let alone her loved ones.

How long could she continue living in this perpetual state of hope? A week? A month? Three months?

If Michael hadn't fallen in love with her by now, would he ever?

"Do you have any suggestions as to how she might meet a gentleman?" Aunt Eleanor asked, returning Tibby's attention to the topic at hand.

"Unfortunately, no." Tibby was the last person who should attempt such a feat when she didn't have a husband. Then again, it would've been impossible to consider the attention of another man when her affection was already taken by Michael.

"The idea holds merit but sounds challenging." Aunt Eleanor's brow furrowed as she mulled over the possibilities. "I suppose the first step is convincing her to attend a function where she might meet someone."

"Hearing your opinion is most helpful. Whether we'll be able to act remains to be seen." The more Tibby considered the details, the more difficult any attempt to execute it sounded.

"Sometimes opening one's eyes to the possibility allows a solution to present itself." Aunt Eleanor sent Tibby a pointed look. "I'm certain you've already experienced serendipitous events in your life."

Joining the Mayfair Literary League was certainly one of those. If Tibby hadn't mentioned her love of reading to Phoebe, who'd then invited her to attend a meeting, Tibby wouldn't have the friends she did. Nor would she have read so many interesting books and enjoyed the discussions they'd had.

She'd grown as a person and expanded her mind with the help of the league. More importantly, she never would've considered taking action to help Michael see her in a new way if not for the group.

Regardless of whether that was successful, she'd had more special moments with him than she had anticipated—moments that she'd carry with her for the rest of her life.

Might the league members also be able to help with her mother? Perhaps they knew of a man near her mother's age who might prove to be a suitable companion, if nothing else.

"I shall ask the members of the Mayfair Literary League," she told her aunt. "They might know someone or perhaps even have a relative who might be of interest to Mother."

"Excellent idea," Aunt Eleanor declared with a nod. "Already the stars are aligning for your idea."

Couldn't she claim that they'd also aligned for her own plan since she was now betrothed to Michael even if it was pretend? Would her luck hold and allow them a chance for a future together?

Doubts rose in her mind as quickly as the questions had. She couldn't think of anything more she could do to make her dream a reality other than stay the course.

"When is your next league meeting?" her aunt asked.

"Tomorrow." The thought brought a wave of nerves. She would be expected to provide an update on her attempt at the *For Better or Worse* agenda.

She felt far from victorious despite what might look like success to others. At least she'd made her move and could take satisfaction in that. Yet somehow, satisfaction was no longer enough.

TIBBY ENTERED HARRIET'S drawing room the following afternoon with anticipation, looking forward to seeing her friends.

Harriet was hosting since Phoebe was still gone. Though they'd debated whether to hold a meeting without their fearless leader, Phoebe had insisted they proceed before she'd departed. Tibby had come early to help Harriet with any last-minute details.

Tibby was grateful Harriet had volunteered to have the meeting. Tibby's mother wouldn't appreciate having guests while she was still recovering. Then again, she didn't appreciate having guests even when she was feeling well.

"Thank you for coming early," Harriet said, her smile warm and kind. As always, her friend wore a high-necked gown. This one was a deep plum that flattered her blonde hair and creamy skin.

"The pleasure is mine," Tibby said as she squeezed Harriet's arm. "Thank you again for allowing us to meet here."

"I've been looking forward to it. I thought we would have refreshments after the meeting since that is what Phoebe normally does."

"Perfect. Are any new members attending?"

They'd had significant interest from ladies to join the group, much to their surprise. Their plan for each member to catch a man's eye had inadvertently been overheard, causing quite the turmoil, especially for Phoebe.

Although they'd expected most people to poke fun at their efforts, that hadn't been the only result. They'd received numerous requests to become a member.

However, it had quickly become clear that many of the ladies were only interested in the *For Better or Worse* agenda and not because of a love of books. Turning away potential members had been a new experience, but reading was the priority of the league and always would be.

"We will have one new guest, Lady Marian Foster. She is an avid reader and even managed to read the book we'll be discussing today. Have you met her?"

"No, I haven't." Considering Tibby had only attended two balls the entire Season, that came as no surprise.

"I'm sure you'll like her. I am anxious to hear how your pretend betrothal is going," Harriet said with a sparkle in her eyes. "Captain Shaw is so handsome and the two of you seem perfect together. But I won't make you tell me since you'll be sharing it with the group soon. Phoebe suggested we ask who would like to be the next to move forward with their agenda after you've shared your experience."

"Excellent idea." Tibby was pleased as that would take some of the pressure off her.

Tibby noted the color that rose in Harriet's cheeks and studied her more closely. "Are you thinking of volunteering?"

Harriet pressed both hands to her face and drew a deep breath. "I will admit only to you that I am considering it. There is a gentleman who has held my attention for some time. I do believe the day has come to help him see me with fresh eyes."

"How exciting," Tibby exclaimed. "I would guess that you're nervous and excited at the same time."

Harriet laughed. "You've described it perfectly."

"Allow me to assure you that what you're experiencing sounds familiar."

Harriet held a hand to her stomach as if to settle the nerves there. "In all honesty, I'm not sure if I have the courage to do it. Or even what 'it' would be."

Tibby nodded. "That is why the support of the group is so important. I could not have done it without all of you. Your encouragement has meant the world to me."

Harriet grinned. "I hope that means you have news to share. I can't wait to hear more."

Tibby assisted her in moving the chairs in the drawing room into a circle, something they found helped to promote discussion. Within a few minutes, the other members arrived.

They had read a compelling mystery this month by a new author, which was another reason Tibby had thought to suggest to Michael that he write one. The story had been enjoyable, but not one of her favorites.

She did not doubt that Michael could do better and was thrilled he'd started work on a story. He hadn't been in touch since their ride in Hyde Park two days ago, but perhaps he was busy. She hoped that was the reason behind his absence.

Harriet called the meeting to order and discussion on the book began.

Most agreed with Tibby. The book held their interest but many of them guessed the murderer's identity within the first three chapters.

"I prefer stories where I am certain I know who the villain is only to realize it has to be someone else several times as

I'm progressing through the book," Winifred said. "That is probably asking too much."

They all agreed they liked the setting, an antique bookshop, and how much they'd like the chance to visit it.

Lady Marian was quite friendly and shared a few thoughts on the book as well. She was near their age with dark hair and bright blue eyes. Tibby already liked her.

At last, Harriet announced their next book selection then looked at Tibby. "Would you care to provide an update on your *For Better or Worse* mission?"

"I have made progress." The excited murmur of voices had her pausing for a moment. "However, I can't call it a success."

"May I ask what you did specifically?" Winifred asked.

Tibby told them of the pretend betrothal, which garnered more excited comments.

Harriet nodded in approval, her expression thoughtful. "Well done. Pretending to be betrothed means pretending to care for one another. What better way to help him see you differently?"

Tibby's cheeks heated as their numerous kisses came to mind. "We shall see what comes of it. There has been one noteworthy drawback that I confess I didn't fully consider. Neither of us like deceiving our family and friends."

More discussion ensued. While all could see the problem, most agreed it was worth the risk. Tibby had yet to know for certain. She didn't think she would until the plan drew to a conclusion, one way or another.

When the conversation paused, Tibby was more than ready to change the subject. "I'm trying to encourage my mother to attend more events. Do any of you know an eligible gentleman her age?"

"Matchmaking?" Harriet grinned. "Excellent idea. My uncle must be close to her age. He's a widower who now lives in London. We could certainly introduce them and see what happens."

"My father's cousin is a widower as well," Lady Marion added. "I'm sure we could arrange a meeting to see if they might suit."

"Excellent. Thank you both." Tibby was pleased and relieved. "I'll be in touch once I find an event my mother is willing to attend."

"Now for the final item on our agenda," Harriet began with a nervous look at Tibby. "Who will be the next to move forward with *For Better or Worse*?"

Harriet lifted her hand from her lap, but before she raised it fully, Frances jerked to her feet. "I would like to try."

Tibby didn't miss the crestfallen look on Harriet's face. Her friend quickly recovered and rose to hug Frances, offering encouragement, along with the other members.

Once refreshments were served and the ladies were visiting, Tibby moved close to Harriet. "Just because Frances is proceeding doesn't mean you have to wait."

"I know. But maybe this is a sign that I should think further on the matter." Indecision clouded Harriet's eyes.

"Don't think too long," Tibby advised in a whisper. "Remember, we don't want to live with regret."

Harriet nodded even as she worried her lip. "True. But this is probably for the best. I don't even have a plan yet."

"You will soon. Be prepared to take a leap of faith when the opportunity presents itself."

Tibby had no idea whether there was hope for her and Michael, but she was pleased she'd taken her own leap. Where it would lead, she still couldn't begin to guess.

MICHAEL RETURNED HOME five days later, exhausted but satisfied with the journey. He and Major Winters, along with two other men they knew from their time in the army, had transported the documents safely and securely. Michael had been grateful for Winters' detailed planning as on two different occasions, they'd faced danger.

First, two rough-looking men had approached them in the stables at the inn where they'd stopped for the night and insisted they take the satchel Winters carried.

Winters had coolly advised them that he would not, under any circumstances, hand it over. Luckily, Jacoby, one of the other men who'd accompanied them, had seen what was happening and managed to surprise the pair from behind with a weapon in hand and chased off the men.

The encounter had them all sleeping with one eye open that evening. They'd taken turns guarding the satchel each night after that.

They were nearing Manchester when the second incident occurred. Michael successfully disarmed the man who tried to rob them at gunpoint but was more shaken than he'd like to admit. It had been some time since he'd faced the wrong end of a gun barrel in such close quarters, and although he had confidence in himself and his companions, he didn't care to repeat the experience.

He was pleased Winters had planned the trip with the proper precautions in place. If not, the journey might've ended much differently.

"I'll send your payment tomorrow," Winters told Michael when they returned to London. "I hope you will join me again if, or should I say when, I receive another request for secure transport. I can't think of anyone I'd rather have at my side."

Michael shook Winters' hand but didn't make any promises. While the mission had given him the purpose he'd been lacking since his return home, at least temporarily, repeating the experience held little appeal.

On the other hand, the thought of being home, seeing Tibby, and working on his book had sounded better with each mile that took them from London.

He'd had significant time to think about Tibby while they were on the road. He could no longer deny his growing feelings for her. He missed her with a deep ache, something that surprised him.

He hesitated to claim he loved her, but his heart suggested otherwise. The idea of any other woman in his life was impossible to consider. Tibby was perfect, and he couldn't believe how long it had taken him to realize that. He intended to show her that he was the right man for her and convince her their betrothal didn't need to be pretend.

"Michael, how nice to have you home," his mother greeted him when he entered the drawing room.

"I'm pleased to be back." At the major's insistence for secrecy, Michael had told his family that he was visiting a fellow officer who lived out of town for a few days. Winters hadn't even told his wife the truth. However, the situation with Tibby had already shown Michael that he didn't care for subterfuge.

"How was your trip?" his mother asked.

He hesitated before answering. Considering the danger he'd been in, it seemed best to keep the details to himself.

His mother wouldn't like it. His grandmother would think him a fool for putting himself in peril when he had only just returned home. She wasn't wrong.

"It was enjoyable, if rather tiring." He bent to kiss her cheek. "How have you and Grandmother fared without me?"

"We managed," she said with a smile. "However, we missed you dearly. We called on Lady Dunford yesterday."

"I'm pleased to hear that. How is she?" What Michael really wanted to know was how Tibby was. The anticipation of seeing her soon set his heart pounding.

"She is much improved and in good spirits. I think we may have convinced her to accompany us to a garden party early next week."

"That is excellent news. Thank you, Mother." He was certain Tibby wouldn't agree to marry him until the situation with her mother had improved. How delightful that his mother was helping to resolve it. "I am sure Tibby appreciated both your visit and the invitation as well."

"Yes, although she seemed surprised to hear you had left for a few days. Didn't you mention it to her?" His mother's frown clearly showed her disapproval of his lack of communication.

Guilt filled Michael. He should've told her. Of course, she'd wonder where he'd gone. It was just that there was so much unspoken between them that he hadn't been ready to address.

"I should have. An oversight on my part. I will call on her as soon as I change."

His mother's frown remained in place. "Is all well between the two of you?"

"Yes." He heaved a sigh, weary of his own uncertainty. "I suppose I thought some time apart might be helpful for both of us."

"I see." Then his mother shook her head. "Actually, I don't. But I trust you know that you can speak with me if I can help."

"I appreciate that, Mother." He reached out to squeeze her hand. "I'm going to make myself presentable and then call on her."

Within a half hour, he'd washed off the dust from his travels and donned clean clothes. He paused by his desk, smiling at the thick pile of notes he had on his novel and the gloves that sat beside them. Anticipation swirled through him as he strode to the front door of Dunford House and knocked.

"I'm sorry, Captain, but Lady Tabitha is not at home. We do expect her to return within the hour," the butler advised him.

Disappointment filled him, the depth of it unsettling. "Please let her know I called."

"Of course."

He returned home but already knew he wouldn't rest until he spoke to Tibby. He only hoped he could show her how much he cared and that a true betrothal might be the perfect solution for them both.

Chapter Sixteen

"Captain Shaw called earlier, Lady Tabitha," the butler advised her upon her return home from the lending library where she'd found a few more books to read to her mother.

Relief filled her at the news only to be quickly smothered. The fact that Michael had left for nearly a week and not bothered to tell her was disheartening. His calling now could mean anything. Perhaps he was having second thoughts and was ready to end their betrothal.

When his mother had mentioned the trip, Tibby hadn't been able to hide her surprise. He hadn't mentioned it during their ride in Hyde Park.

Or had that outing been the reason he'd decided to leave for a few days?

The worry was thoroughly depressing.

Did she send word that she was home or wait for him to call again?

"Also, Mrs. Cameron said Lady Dunford's stomach was bothering her again and requested one of your remedies," the butler added.

"Of course." Tibby didn't have time to wonder how to proceed. The next two hours were taken with preparing a mint and ginger tea and caring for her mother alongside her aunt.

Alice slipped Tibby a message as evening drew near. Tibby opened it with trembling fingers, certain who had sent it.

Meet me in the greenhouse in the coming hour. If not, come in the morning, if your schedule permits.

M

She reread the words three times but still couldn't guess his intention. Deciding it would be best if she met with him now rather than worrying all night about what he might say, she left Aunt Eleanor with her mother and fetched a shawl from her room, not bothering to put on gloves.

Hoping no one watched her leave, she stepped out the garden door then took a moment to let the fresh air and the sight of the garden soothe her.

Her mother's illness meant she hadn't spent as much time in the gardens as she liked. Already she could see the herb and vegetable beds needed tending. Perhaps tomorrow she'd have time to do some work.

She passed through the gate that separated their garden from Michael's and saw a faint glow of light coming from the greenhouse.

Reminding herself not to borrow trouble, she fixed a smile on her face and opened the door. At the very least, she wanted to ask why he hadn't told her he was leaving town.

Humid air scented by flowers and soil filled the small space. She set aside her shawl, already warm. "Michael?"

"In the back," he called out.

She rounded a corner and saw him standing before the work table in only his shirt sleeves. His hair was mussed, a smudge of dirt on one cheek.

Drat, she thought. He was especially appealing when he looked disheveled as if she needed to be further tempted by him.

He glanced up and smiled, one hand holding two parts of a stem together in a pot as he attempted to tuck soil around the base. "I don't suppose you'd be willing to lend a hand?"

"Of course." Her heart lightened at his smile and his bright eyes. Surely both boded well for his mood and the purpose of their conversation. "Doing another graft?"

"Only because an earlier one failed." He sighed. "Botany is definitely not my calling."

She stepped close to his side, so near that she could feel the warmth of his body and catch the scent of his cologne as she reached for the stem. Her knees weakened as desire stirred. She forced herself to focus on the plant. "It appears to almost be in place."

"If you could hold the stems together, I'll put the soil in the pot to keep it there."

She moved even closer, pressing against his upper arm to do so. A slow breath did little to ease her awareness. Not when that breath only drew in more of his woodsy scent. If she didn't know better, she'd think his cologne was an elixir of sorts to lure her even closer.

Her gaze held on his forearm, so masculine with its sculpted muscles and covering of dark hair. His movements had a certain grace as he patted the soil around the base of the plant.

She was obviously the only one experiencing this awareness as Michael's focus was on his work. The lamp on the far end of the table showed how long his lashes were, a stark contrast to the rest of his masculine appeal. His hair looked freshly washed and held a slight curl, one of which fell over his forehead. Done with the plant, he stepped to a bucket of water and rinsed his hands before returning to wipe them on a nearby towel.

"Clearly, I should've requested your assistance when I first started these experiments," he said as he glanced at her. Then he looked again, longer this time. His eyes darkened as his focus shifted.

To her.

She bit her lower lip, trying to tamp down any signs of what she was feeling from appearing on her face. As if her uneven breath and flushed cheeks wouldn't make it evident.

His gaze dropped to her mouth, and her heartbeat thundered.

With a muttered oath, he tossed aside the towel and reached for her, kissing her with a masterfulness that caused her bones to melt.

"Tibby," he whispered between kisses, pulling her tightly against him. "I missed you so."

She tried to gather her thoughts and provide a reply. She had a question, she remembered. If only she could think of what it was. Yet as he nibbled below her ear and down her neck, she became certain it could wait.

After first winding her arms around his shoulders, she shifted to run her fingers over his neck and through his thick hair.

The feel of his lips along her collarbone made her grateful for the lower neckline of the gown she happened to wear. Her breasts tingled, seeming eager for his touch.

She blinked. How wanton of her.

"I thought of you so often while I was gone." He took her lips again, his tongue spearing into her mouth as if he were intent on devouring her.

His words slowly sank in. This was her chance to ask him where he'd gone. Why hadn't he told her? But she couldn't force out the words. Not when they might end this sweet torture.

She ran her hands over those broad shoulders, feeling each corded muscle through the fine linen of his shirt. His thick chest beckoned next. When he moaned as her fingers caught in the opening of his shirt, she took that as a sign to explore further.

"Each time I see you, I only want you more." He drew back to look into her eyes.

"You do?" She couldn't quite grasp that. He couldn't possibly feel the same way she did.

"So much." He squeezed her waist, his hands moving up to her ribs until his thumbs perched just below her breasts.

Her nipples tightened, and she could hardly breathe. Please, she wanted to beg. Please touch me.

As if reading her thoughts, his fingers traced the neckline of her gown, dipping inside the fabric. A shiver ran along her skin, and she arched back.

"Yes," he murmured and reached inside the gown to caress her breast, gently plucking the tip, sending an arrow of need shooting straight through her.

Bolder now, she reached inside his shirt, loving the feel of his warm skin. The coarse hair on his chest was a pleasant surprise and made her wish he'd take off his shirt so she could better see him.

"Tibby, I want to touch you everywhere."

Her breath caught as he pulled his hand free to take hold of her waist and lift her onto the work table as if she weighed no more than a feather.

He parted her knees to stand between them and kissed her once again. It took a moment for her to note the feel of his fingers on her calf, gliding along her stocking. Her body filled with liquid heat at his gentle touch, especially when he lingered at the back of her knee.

Why that spot was so sensitive, she couldn't begin to guess. It made her wonder what other places were as well. It was as if Michael had a compass to guide him unerringly to the areas of her body that stole her breath. That made her ache with need.

When his hand grazed her inner thigh, she gasped.

"I need to touch you, Tabitha."

His use of her full name added to the headiness of the moment.

"Oh, Michael," was nearly more than she could manage. "Yes. Please."

The apex between her thighs pulsed as if helping to guide him. She'd read about moments like this. But never had she believed herself capable of feeling so passionate. Of wanting his touch with every cell of her body. Of desire pushing away her inhibitions.

His fingers brushed her cotton drawers and made her wish she wasn't wearing any. Yet the thin barrier didn't stop him. He easily found their slit and brushed against the curls there. Once. Twice.

She broke off the kiss, unable to catch her breath. Her body throbbed. There was no other way to describe it.

He shifted, spreading her knees open wider, leaving her feeling vulnerable. His fingers explored the flesh there, finding her damp folds and caressing them.

Should she be alarmed by how wet she felt? Before she could worry, he pressed his fingers against her very center, massaging the entrance even as he took her mouth with his once again.

He continued the intimate caresses until all thought was gone, and she could only feel each stroke, her body swaying to the rhythm he set.

"Come for me, Tibby," Michael whispered. "Let go."

She frowned, uncertain of what he meant until her entire body tightened as if she teetered on a precipice. Then she flew, convulsing as she soared. She could only hold onto Michael for dear life as her world shattered.

When the last shudder settled into a mere shiver, Michael leaned back to look at her. "You are beautiful." He kissed her again, his tongue repeating the same rhythm.

She blinked as tears threatened. At that moment, she felt beautiful and more of a woman than she had her entire life. "Michael," she whispered. He was a sorcerer. That was the only explanation for the magic he'd made her feel.

"Tabitha." He smiled even as he straightened the skirts of her gown. "We shouldn't linger in here too long." Then he took hold of her waist, prepared to lift her to the ground. "Ready?"

No. She wasn't. She had no desire to leave this cozy space even if a pot on the back of the table was digging into her hip. But she only nodded.

He set her on the ground but continued to hold her. His gentle kiss eased her reluctance.

Based on the books she'd read, she knew he had needs as well. She glanced down, noting his taut trousers, and reached to touch the hardness there. "Can I provide you with...pleasure as well?" Speaking of these things was more difficult than she could've imagined.

Michael half-laughed and half-groaned then pressed his manhood into her hand a moment before easing back. "Not this time. The longer we're in here, the more the chance we might be discovered."

He glanced at the stems scattered on the work table. "I think the graft will have to wait for another day." He faced her again and tucked a strand of hair behind her ear. "I'm sorry I didn't mention I was leaving for a few days. I went to aid a friend, and the matter came up rather quickly."

"I see."

"Can you forgive me for not saying goodbye?"

If you promise not to do so again. She'd been terribly hurt by his departure. The fact that he'd apologized eased her upset, but his leaving the way he had served as a reminder that this was all still pretend.

Whatever was between them was fragile—a house built of straw.

The fragility was becoming more difficult to endure. Especially when she wanted so much more.

"Of course."

"Mother tells me that she invited your mother to a garden party. Do you think she'll attend?"

"I hope so. Aunt Eleanor and I are determined that she does." How was she supposed to carry on a coherent conversation after what he'd just made her feel?

"Perhaps we can all go."

"I'd like that." Having something to look forward to with Michael helped to ease the knot of worry that seemed permanently bound around her heart.

Surely what had just happened meant there was hope. That one day soon, he would truly be hers.

MICHAEL MET WITH MARKUS'S solicitor two days later. His brother spoke highly of the man.

"He has a golden touch when it comes to investments," Markus had promised when Michael mentioned his hope of using the payment he'd received from Winters to earn more.

"I suppose now that you're about to become a married man, you're thinking more seriously about the future," Markus had said.

"Yes, I suppose I am." His pretend betrothal to Tibby was turning very real. The interlude in the greenhouse had confirmed how well-suited they were for one another in every possible way.

Watching her come apart in his arms had nearly undone him. He'd spent a tortured night after that, and not even working on his novel had distracted him from the need that made his body ache.

If he wanted to make the situation with Tibby permanent, it was imperative that he make plans for his future.

Mr. Johnson had several suggestions for Michael to consider that should pay handsomely in the near term. While the investments held risk, it wasn't as significant as others.

"Allow me to think about it for a day or two before I decide," Michael had advised the man.

The next item on his list was to find a suitable place to live with the hope Tibby would eventually join him there. He couldn't stay with his mother for much longer. While he'd enjoyed her and his grandmother's company, he wanted some privacy.

However, that meant moving away from Tibby. The thought had him hesitating. He hoped for another interlude in the greenhouse if possible.

He paused on the pavement outside the solicitor's office. Was he prepared to marry her? Would she have him if he proposed in truth? With so little to offer her, he didn't know the answer. Would the promise of more to come be enough?

With a heavy sigh, he continued to the club where he'd arranged to meet his brother for a drink. He almost wished he hadn't, given the way his thoughts were churning.

"How did your meeting go?" Markus asked when Michael joined him at a table. "What did you think of Johnson?"

"He was very helpful," Michael said.

"Then why the somber face?" Markus asked. "Having doubts about the wedding?" He frowned. "Have you even set a date yet or discussed the marriage settlement?"

"Not yet."

"Dragging your feet, eh?" Markus nodded. "It's a big step. I felt much the same way even after I proposed to Victoria."

That didn't help Michael when his situation was different. Unique. He wasn't about to tell his brother the betrothal was only pretend, but he now thought he wanted it to be real.

His brother would think him crazy, and Michael couldn't blame him.

Markus leaned forward, the teasing glint in his eyes fading. "It comes down to a few simple questions. Can you imagine your future without her? Are you happier when you're with her or by yourself? And lastly, how would you feel if you saw her in the arms of another? When you can answer those, you know."

If that were true, then he already knew his answer.

Chapter Seventeen

Despite Aunt Eleanor dropping hints about returning home, Tibby asked her to stay at least until after the garden party as she would need all the help she could get to convince her mother to attend.

Of course, having Lady Trafford invite her mother made the process easier, but Tibby knew from experience that she might change her mind at the last minute. She had done that too many times to count in the last few years.

Tibby and her aunt helped to select a bright blue gown for Tibby's mother to wear, hoping it would further brighten her spirits. They'd agreed to express as much excitement for the event as possible with the hope it would encourage her mother to feel the same.

Harriet had sent a message telling Tibby that her uncle agreed to accompany her and her mother, Lady Chapman, to the party, so they could all be introduced. Tibby hadn't said a word to her mother, but Aunt Eleanor knew and was in full support of the plan.

Once they'd settled in the carriage the day of the party, Tibby heaved a quiet sigh of relief, sharing a smile with Aunt Eleanor that they'd managed this. Their carriage followed Michael, his mother, and his grandmother, who rode in their conveyance, toward Brighton House.

The day was warm and sunny—perfect for an afternoon in a garden. While Tibby hoped her mother enjoyed the outing and that she liked Harriet's uncle, her own excitement centered on the chance to be with Michael.

Her cheeks heated at the thought of their interlude in the greenhouse. How could she possibly act as if nothing had happened after that?

"Is something amiss, Tabitha?" her mother asked, her far-too-observant gaze holding on Tibby's flushed cheeks.

"Not at all." She waved a hand before her face and looked out the window. "It's a rather warm day, isn't it?"

What if Aunt Eleanor and her mother somehow realized what had happened between her and Michael? The worry was a silly one, but she couldn't help it. Not when she felt so different after those moments in Michael's arms. The experience made her even more curious about making love with him. Would she ever have the chance?

They soon arrived at Brighton House, and Michael assisted them to alight.

"Thank you, Captain Shaw." Tibby's mother gave him a warm smile.

"My pleasure," Michael said, sharing a surprised look with Tibby as he then handed down her aunt followed by Tibby. "Excuse me while I assist my grandmother."

"Of course," Tibby said. His gallantry was one of the many reasons she admired him. She had no doubt his grandmother appreciated it as well. The older woman's beaming smile as Michael took her arm made that clear.

The group exchanged pleasantries as they walked up the steps to the elegant house where a liveried footman welcomed them before escorting their group through the richly appointed home to the gardens where Lord and Lady Brighton greeted guests.

Lady Trafford took her mother-in-law's arm so they could speak with their hosts, leaving Michael to return to Tibby.

He took her hand and tucked it beneath his elbow. "I hope the day finds you well." The heated glint in his eyes suggested that he was thinking of their time in the greenhouse.

"It does," she replied, feeling her cheeks warm once again. How could they not when he looked at her so intently? "And you?"

"Much better now that I'm with you."

She looked at him in surprise, touched by his words.

His eyes narrowed. "Why do you always seem shocked when I say something of that sort?" He pressed her hand tighter against his side. "I enjoy spending time with you. That shouldn't come as a surprise."

She gave a small shake of her head. "Yet it does." She'd never had someone say such nice things to her. She was beginning to think he wasn't merely pretending.

"It shouldn't be," he replied. "You have always been excellent company and my appreciation for that has only increased since we became betrothed."

Tibby caught herself as she started to deny it. If the last few weeks had taught her anything, it was that she needed to embrace moments like this. Who was she to argue if he said he enjoyed being with her? "Thank you. I enjoy your company as well."

"I also look forward to the next time we can *thoroughly* enjoy each other's company." His teasing grin suggested he referred to the greenhouse again.

She couldn't help but laugh. "You're incorrigible."

He leaned close to whisper in her ear, "Grafting might become my favorite pastime after all if I can do it with you." He wiggled his brows suggestively, and her cheeks practically burned with embarrassment.

With courage she didn't realize she had, she matched his grin and added what she hoped was a suggestive look of her own. "Mine as well."

His startled reaction pleased her. This daring side of her might be unfamiliar, but it was delightful to feel feminine power.

She had promised herself to help him see her in a new light, and based on his expression, she'd done just that once again.

His eyes darkened, confirming it.

"Michael," his mother called.

They both looked up to see they'd fallen behind the rest of their group, which was already entering the terraced garden.

After they greeted their hosts then walked forward to join the others, Tibby whispered, "My friend Harriet's widowed uncle is here, and I hope to introduce him to my mother."

Michael studied her again. "You are full of surprises today."

"I don't know whether it will work. But it's certainly worth a try. Perhaps the attention of a gentleman will provide her with something other than her illnesses to think about."

"Brilliant," Michael said with admiration. "It seems that you didn't need my assistance after all."

Surely it wasn't concern that furrowed his brow.

Before they could speak further, they were greeted by other guests. Tibby saw Harriet and her mother a short distance away, standing with a distinguished-looking gentleman.

He was well-groomed, fit, and handsome for a man his age. His grey hair, with a slightly receding hairline, and an intelligent yet friendly face gave her a good feeling. Her hope for the situation rose a little higher. Maybe this was possible.

She smiled at Harriet, who returned it with an encouraging nod. That must mean her uncle was amiable to the situation. She dearly hoped so.

Michael accompanied her as she crossed the terrace to greet Harriet. "Michael, you remember my friend, Lady Harriet."

"Of course. It's a pleasure to see you again." He offered a bow and a charming smile.

"Captain Shaw." Harriet smiled. "It's a lovely day, isn't it?" Her questioning look as she glanced between Tibby and Michael made Tibby wonder what she saw.

Tibby couldn't deny that Michael's attentiveness felt all too real as if they truly were a couple.

Again, her hopes rose, but this time for herself. Surely this wasn't merely an act on his part. Those moments in the greenhouse hadn't felt like one either. If he desired her, was that one step closer to love? The question sent her emotions spinning, and she drew a deep breath to clear her thoughts.

Seemingly unaware of the mayhem tumbling through Tibby, Harriet lifted a brow, clearly ready to proceed with the introduction.

Tibby glanced over her shoulder and caught Aunt Eleanor's attention. Her aunt reached for her mother's arm and gestured to where they stood.

The two joined them, and Tibby did her best to act casually. "Mother, you remember my friend Lady Harriet and her mother, Lady Chapman."

"Good afternoon." Her mother offered a polite smile.

Tibby continued, "This is my aunt, Mrs. Eleanor Cameron, who is visiting for a few weeks."

"May I introduce my uncle, Mr. Matthew Hancock," Harriet added.

"A pleasure, ladies," the gentleman said warmly, and Tibby couldn't have been more pleased by the interested glint in her mother's eyes.

The conversation continued for several minutes with Tibby and Michael contributing little. Aunt Eleanor stepped away to speak with an acquaintance while Harriet and Lady Chapman remained nearby but spoke to each other.

Much to Tibby's surprise, her mother spoke animatedly to Mr. Hancock, responding to his questions with an uncharacteristic friendliness. The pink in her mother's cheeks was delightful to see.

Deciding it best to leave them to become better acquainted without an audience, Tibby looked at Michael. "Would you care for a stroll?"

"Anywhere with you," he replied, his eyes warm.

Tibby's heart grew just a little bit bigger, something she would've insisted was impossible when she already cared so much for this man.

Was this love? Unequivocally, yes.

She pressed a single finger to her chest when her heart thumped alarmingly. She reminded herself to enjoy this time but keep her hope within reasonable measures.

They had just stepped away when Tibby caught sight of Lady Lucinda and her sister, Lady Jane, greeting their hosts.

Tibby groaned.

"What is it?" Michael followed her gaze. "The two sisters from the ball. Not exactly friends of yours, are they?"

"No. I can't say that I care for them."

Tibby turned away, and she and Michael walked toward a nearby flower bed, which held various roses. Several minutes later, Tibby looked to see how her mother was faring, only to see Lady Lucinda speaking with Harriet.

That couldn't be a good thing.

"I should see if Harriet needs assistance," Tibby told Michael. Her friend's brow furrowed, her shoulders growing stiff.

"She looks rather distraught," he agreed as he offered his arm. "Your mother seems upset by the conversation as well."

Aunt Eleanor returned to the group just as Tibby and Michael joined them.

"That isn't true." Her mother's voice raised in a shrill tone that didn't bode well. Her gaze shifted to Tibby, alarm in her expression. "Tabitha, tell her she's wrong."

Tibby's stomach tightened as she looked from her unhappy mother to Harriet's outrage to Lady Lucinda's smugness.

The latter was the most concerning sight of all.

Oh dear.

Before Tibby could ask what had been said, Lady Lucinda reached out to touch her arm, as if sharing a confidence. "I merely asked Harriet if she intended to propose to a man as Lady Phoebe did. I assume you did the same, as well."

Her words sent Tibby's stomach plunging as if she'd toppled over the edge of a waterfall with no boat. Why hadn't she anticipated that this could happen given that the news of their agenda had spread even before Phoebe had married?

"Tell her that's a lie, Tabitha," her mother demanded. "You wouldn't have proposed to Captain Shaw."

"Isn't that how the Mayfair Literary League works?" Lady Jane asked with feigned innocence. "Instead of waiting for a gentleman to ask you to marry him, you ladies are the ones doing the asking."

Harriet shook her head, her eyes flashing with anger. "That is not what the *For Better or Worse* agenda is at all."

Michael stared at Tibby, the dark shadow of doubt in his expression. "To what is she referring?"

Tibby couldn't catch her breath. One moment, she and Michael had been enjoying a lovely afternoon, and the next, everything was unraveling before her eyes.

"Yes," Tibby's mother added. "Explain yourself."

Michael's mother joined them, her brow furrowed as she stared between Tibby and Michael. "Surely, this doesn't have anything to do with your betrothal. You proposed to Lady Tabitha, didn't you, Michael?"

Michael's lips tightened. "Not exactly."

Lady Lucinda's gleeful look made Tibby want to crawl under the nearby boxwood hedge to hide. "You *did* propose to the captain." The lady clapped her hands twice. "Just as I suspected. Do you really intend to marry or is it some sort of ploy?"

Lady Trafford frowned as she glanced between Tibby and Michael, her doubt obvious. "You have yet to set a date or even discuss making a formal announcement."

"Isn't the betrothal real?" Aunt Eleanor asked with disbelief and disappointment.

Tibby's cheeks burned. How could she possibly explain when everyone was staring? Especially Michael. Her embarrassment only served to make her look guilty in everyone's eyes, from Michael to her mother to Aunt Eleanor, not to mention his mother.

Before she could form an answer, Michael said, "You made the suggestion as part of the book group rather than out of true need?"

"What need would that be?" Lady Trafford asked.

"This isn't what it sounds like," Tibby began.

"Tabitha, I insist we leave immediately." Her mother sniffed. "I refuse to endure another moment of this." She met Lady Trafford's gaze. "I must apologize for my daughter's behavior. I can't imagine what she was thinking."

"Wait!" Tibby held up her hand as she glanced around the group, well aware they'd drawn attention from the other guests as well. She turned to Michael first. "Please let me explain. I never meant to hurt you."

"Then perhaps you should've told me the truth." Michael's quiet words and the pain on his face sent a terrible fear spiraling through her. "I thought we were friends, but it seems I was only convenient." He started to turn away only to turn back. "Actually, I thought we were more than friends."

Tears filled Tibby's eyes. "Michael, please. We are. Allow me to explain."

"Not now." He shook his head. "Not yet. I need time to think."

"Michael—" his mother began.

"Take the carriage," he told her. "I'll find my own way home."

With that, he stalked away as if his feet couldn't carry him quickly enough, taking Tibby's heart with him.

Chapter Eighteen

Michael strode out of Brighton House, completely ignoring the startled servants he passed as well as the other guests who were arriving. He didn't see any of them. He only knew he needed to get away as quickly as possible.

He couldn't for the life of him understand what had just happened. He'd thought he and Tibby were coming to an understanding about a possible future together, something they both might want.

At least, *he* had wanted that.

He'd also thought she needed his help. That had felt good. More than good. He'd appreciated having a sense of purpose again, albeit temporarily. Assisting her to loosen Lady Dunford's grasp was supposed to give Tibby the chance for a future of her own desire.

He'd been beginning to hope—to believe—she might want to share that future with him. In fact, he was leaving tomorrow to assist Major Winters on another mission to secure additional funds, so he'd be better prepared financially if that occurred.

To learn that her literary league was the reason behind her approaching him with the idea of a pretend betrothal was disappointing. The ache in his chest said it was more than disappointing. He was hurt.

He'd merely been convenient. An easy target for her plan since they were already friends. Why hadn't Tibby told him the truth?

"Michael! Michael, wait. Please."

His pace slowed and he reluctantly turned back to see Tibby hurrying toward him.

"Allow me to explain," she said breathlessly. "It's not what you think."

The sight of her was enough to cause his heart to trip. Despite what he'd just learned, he cared for Tibby and wanted a future with her. No one else would do.

"Did you suggest the betrothal because of the literary league?" he asked. He didn't appreciate being used for some crazy scheme presented by her book group.

He much preferred the idea that she needed him. The purpose her request had given him had changed his life for the better.

Her lips parted only to close as if she needed time to think of an answer. That was an answer in itself as far as he was concerned.

He shook his head, more disappointed than he could say.

"The league only encourages its members to act if they hold affection for someone."

Affection? As in friendship? He'd hoped Tibby felt more for him than that. But the concern would have to wait. Whether or not she realized it, she needed him now. "Never mind. The damage has already been done. All that matters is what was said in front of those two ladies who are so clearly intent on stirring trouble."

"I'll speak with them. They might listen to reason. But please know that—"

He stopped her, unable to bear her saying how much their friendship meant. Friendship wasn't enough as far as he was concerned. "We'll talk of it later. Given the circumstances, I think it would be best if we change the terms of our betrothal."

She frowned, clearly puzzled. "How so?"

"When news of this spreads, it will cast a blot on your reputation. There's only one solution. We should marry." He gave a decisive nod. "Soon."

The relief he felt at saying those words fell away when she only stared at him in disbelief. He obviously hadn't said it right.

Panic set in as he tried to better explain himself. "I realize I'm partially at fault for agreeing to the pretend betrothal. By marrying, we will quiet any gossip. It will save your reputation, and all will be well." He expected to feel satisfaction, but something was wrong.

Based on Tibby's cool expression, it was very wrong.

"How kind of you," she said politely, though the distinct chill in her voice was impossible to miss. "But I must refuse."

"Why? I want to protect you. I want to help." He needed to more than he could possibly explain.

"Your offer is very gallant, but no." She smiled, yet it was anything but happy. "That's not a reason to begin a life together. My reputation isn't so important that it requires such a...sacrifice on your part. I do not go about in Society often and losing that privilege will be unfortunate. Hopefully, I will still have my friends. There's no need to concern yourself with protecting me. But thank you for your thoughtfulness."

Thoughtfulness? His heart ached at her words. He wasn't trying to be thoughtful. He was trying to protect her. Why was she refusing his offer of assistance to her own peril?

"How can I help you if you won't let me?" he asked, dumbfounded by her refusal.

"Michael, I wouldn't want you to think of the sacrifice you made each time you look at me in the coming years." She stepped closer, lifting a hand only to let it fall. "If you'd allow me to explain—"

"I think it best that I go since it's clear you no longer need me." He gave a stiff bow and turned on his heel to stride away.

"Michael, wait!"

He ignored her plea, too upset to listen to whatever she had to say. He had to go before he said something that might hurt her. He already hurt enough for them both.

"I WOULD LIKE A WORD with you, Mother," Tibby had said upon their arrival home from the garden party.

She'd tried to explain in the carriage, but her mother refused to listen.

"I'm not interested in anything you have to say," was her reply.

"Perhaps it would be best if we all had time to settle our thoughts before we discuss this further," Aunt Eleanor suggested, her obvious disapproval only making Tibby feel worse.

And so they had all retired to their bedrooms.

Tibby paced the length of hers as numbness took hold, making it impossible to think. All she could see was Michael's hurt and disappointment. His suggestion that they should marry had been a dream come true except for one thing—it was for the wrong reason.

He hadn't offered out of love, but out of duty. That would make for a cold marriage. She had to wonder if he'd understood when she told him the league only encouraged action toward the man for whom they had affection. Perhaps she should've been completely honest and told him how she felt. Would that have made a difference?

While uncertain if she might've had a chance for a future with him before today, she'd hoped they were moving in that direction. To think she'd had everything she wanted in the palm of her hand only to drop it was heart-wrenching.

She should've guessed that something like this might happen, considering Phoebe's experience. That she and Michael had already told Lady Lucinda and Lady Jane about their betrothal without consequence had made her complacent. What had she been thinking?

She didn't know whether she would have the chance to speak to Michael again, but she would at least force her mother to listen. Tibby had no expectation that it would go well.

The afternoon was waning when Tibby asked her aunt to join her when she spoke with her mother.

"I look forward to hearing an explanation," Aunt Eleanor agreed and followed Tibby to her mother's bedroom.

After knocking on the door, she opened it, certain her mother's mood hadn't changed.

"I don't want to hear what you have to say, Tabitha." Her mother lifted her nose in the air from where she sat in a chair by the window. "Your behavior has been deplorable."

"So has yours." Tibby couldn't believe the words escaped her. But while willing to take the blame and apologize to those she'd hurt, she wanted her mother to understand her part in the situation.

"What could you possibly mean?"

Tibby looked at her aunt who now sat on the edge of the bed. "I'm sorry you had to witness the events of the afternoon, but I'm pleased you're here."

"Tabitha—" her mother began.

"I have something to say, and I intend to say it now," Tibby interrupted. Before she lost her confidence. Before the realization that she'd lost Michael sank in.

Her mother stared out the window with her arms folded over her chest, her displeasure clear.

"I've been a member of the Mayfair Literary League for nearly two years and have become dear friends with the other members. We have many things in common, most especially a love of books. But another is the fact that none of us have married. We've all had five Seasons or more but for one reason or another, we haven't found husbands. Therefore, we agreed to do something to help the men for whom we have feelings to see us differently."

"By proposing to them?" Aunt Eleanor's wide eyes suggested she could hardly believe it. "I'm in favor of women's rights, but this seems extreme."

"That was not part of the plan. One of the other members did suggest a marriage of convenience to the man for whom she cared. I'm happy to share that Lady Phoebe recently married that man, and they are both deeply in love."

"Oh. How interesting," Aunt Eleanor said, clearly amazed by that outcome.

"No, it's not. It's terrible." Her mother pressed a hand to her forehead in apparent disbelief. "To think my daughter is so desperate for a husband that she's resorted to trickery to gain one is more than I can bear."

"It wasn't like that." If her own mother couldn't understand, how could she hope Michael would?

She hated that she had deceived him with all this. But it wasn't as if she had taken away his choice. He'd agreed to the pretend betrothal for his own reasons.

Tibby pushed aside those thoughts for the moment and moved to kneel beside her mother's chair, taking her hand only to have her pull it away. Despite the rejection, she hoped her mother would listen. "Mother, you know I love you. But your continual insistence that you're ill along with your preference to remain home and not take part in life is too much."

Her mother's mouth dropped agape. "Are you implying this is somehow my fault? That I'm to blame for your behavior?"

"No. I'm telling you that I can't watch you live like this. Not anymore. The situation isn't healthy for either of us."

"Mary, I have to agree with Tabitha's point," Aunt Eleanor said, her expression sympathetic.

Her mother stiffened with outrage as she returned her focus to Tibby. "Is this why you introduced me to Mr. Hancock? Do you intend to marry me off so you don't have to deal with me anymore?"

Tibby sighed, trying to gather the strength to deal with this when all she wanted to do was find Michael and beg him to understand.

But that wasn't possible and, until then, she needed to try to claim her future, regardless of whether or not that involved Michael. He'd taught her to look at herself in a new way, and for that, she was grateful. She liked who she was when she was with him—someone more. Someone who deserved happiness. The realization had her straightening and finding her courage.

"No, Mother. I arranged an introduction to Mr. Hancock with the hope that you might enjoy his company and he might enjoy yours. I hoped he could remind you that there's more to life than the walls of this house. Father has been gone a long time. I know how much you loved him. I miss him, too, but he would want you to be happy. It's not just that you don't want to go out, but you're displeased if I do," Tibby continued.

"I don't know what you're talking about. You can go wherever you like."

"And you make sure to show your displeasure when I return. That's not fair, Mother."

"I know you don't want to hear this, Mary," Aunt Eleanor added, "but Tabitha is right. I've seen it for myself. You need to get out more. Staying home all the time is not healthy for you and it's not fair to your daughter."

Her mother's chin trembled. "Doesn't it matter what I want?"

"You can't tell me that you're happy." Tibby held her mother's gaze for a long moment, hoping she would see that truth. "All Aunt Eleanor and I want is for you to be happy.

What you think you want isn't working. It's time to try something else."

"So now the two of you have joined forces against me?" Her mother's eyes filled with tears, but she lifted her chin, still defiant. "If I am such a burden, then go. Both of you should leave."

"No," Aunt Eleanor said. "We love you, and we want to help you. But you have to help us as well."

"All we ask is that you try a few new activities," Tibby said. "Let's find an event or two you think you might enjoy. We'll both go if that's what you'd like. For the remainder of the Season, let us try to make new friends or become reacquainted with old ones. Perhaps you'll enjoy spending time with Mr. Hancock, or perhaps you won't. Regardless, you have to make some changes."

"I don't want any of this." Her mother covered her face with trembling hands, her voice barely audible. "I want everything as it used to be. When your father was here, and we were all together. When Victor still loved me, and so did you. I don't want to be alone."

A hot, tight ball of emotion filled Tibby's chest. Nothing was the same nor would it ever be. Hadn't she had those same thoughts? The fear that if she loved someone, she would only lose them. Especially since she and her mother had lost those they loved the most.

Tibby straightened to her knees to hug her mother. "I'm so sorry, Mother," she whispered. "I'm sorry Father died, and Victor married. I'm sorry they left us."

And that I'm not enough to comfort you or make you happy.

Tibby released a silent gasp as that truth rose inside her. She felt it to her core and shuddered at the realization of what had been inside her heart all this time.

She wasn't enough. Not enough to keep her father alive, to stop Michael from leaving, or to keep Victor more involved, let alone to help her mother rediscover happiness.

Even as she acknowledged the thought that had gripped her for so long, part of her—the logical part—saw it for the lie it was.

She *was* enough. It wasn't her fault that her father had died or that Victor had moved on with his life. Of course, Michael had pursued his own path as well. She wouldn't have it any other way.

Most of all, her mother's unhappiness wasn't Tibby's responsibility. Lady Dunford's emotional state was her own choice, and while Tibby would continue to do all in her power to change it, ultimately, it was up to her mother.

Somehow, she needed to release the burden of the heavy weight she'd carried for so long.

"I can't go through that kind of loss again," her mother whispered when she removed her hands to stare at Tibby, the pain in them causing Tibby's eyes to fill with tears as well. "Why should I try?"

"Because love and happiness are worth the risk." As Tibby said the words, she realized what she should have done differently. She should've found a better way to express her feelings to Michael. She should've allowed their relationship to grow naturally, and then told him how she felt.

But she hadn't. Her fear of not being enough had convinced her that her only choice was to devise a ruse for why she wanted to be with him—to deceive him.

Her entire body trembled at the truth. How could he ever forgive her?

As she'd told her mother, love was worth the risk if one dared to reach for it. She'd spent so much time being afraid of losing him that she hadn't trusted the connection they'd shared. She hadn't believed he could truly love her.

Now, she had nothing left to lose. She needed to speak to him and share what was in her heart and ask his forgiveness.

She only hoped he'd listen.

Aunt Eleanor joined them. "The two of you have been through so much. I hope you can both move past this. Tabitha, I can see why you felt you had to do something drastic, but deceiving others is never wise. Mary, I hope you realize it's time for a change. Life is too short not to find happiness where we can."

Tibby's mother sniffed again and took a shuddering breath. "I'm not sure I'm strong enough to try."

"Mother, you are stronger than you know," Tabitha said. "I'm certain of it. We both need to face our fears and embrace life. You will never lose me. I'll always be your daughter. Living fully with joy will bring us closer."

Her mother managed to smile and reached out a hand to cup Tibby's cheek. "I don't know what I did to deserve you, but I am grateful to have you as my daughter."

Tibby leaned forward to kiss her mother's cheek. "I'm lucky to have you as my mother."

The discussion had gone better than she could've hoped. Now, if only she could have the same success with Michael or even a portion of it. Anything would be better than the way they'd parted.

If he couldn't forgive her, the future would be bleak. Barren, in fact, since he held her heart. How could she live without him?

Chapter Nineteen

"He asked you to marry him, and you said no?" Harriet paused to stare at Tibby in surprise.

"He didn't ask. He *suggested* we marry. Out of duty. As a way to protect me and save my reputation." Tibby looped her arm through Harriet's, and they continued along the garden path outside her house.

They hadn't had a chance to talk when Tibby had returned to the garden party before her mother insisted on leaving.

Four long, painful days had passed since that disastrous day. Harriet had called to see how she was faring, something Tibby appreciated. However, Aunt Eleanor had been in the drawing room when Harriet arrived and Tibby wanted to speak with Harriet alone, so they stepped into the garden for some privacy and fresh air.

"It's not that I don't appreciate his kindness..." That's where the offer had come from. Kindness. He hadn't mentioned undying love for her. Or a love of any sort. Of course, he hadn't.

But still...

She couldn't help but glance at his house, her heart aching to know he wasn't there. Alice had discovered from his footman that he'd left on another trip the day after the garden party, but he didn't know where Michael had gone or when he'd return.

"Were you able to explain everything?"

"I tried to, but I should've been more direct and told him how I felt before he left." Then again, if she'd confessed her love for him, would it have made any difference?

"Don't you want to marry him?" Harriet asked, still clearly puzzled.

"More than anything." She swallowed against the tight knot of emotion in her throat, something she'd been doing frequently of late, even after she thought she'd shed every tear she had. "But only for love. Not duty."

Tibby pressed a finger to her temple, exhausted from reviewing the events in her mind and wondering if she'd done the right thing. Should she have agreed and hoped he would come to love her?

No. That hadn't worked with the betrothal and wouldn't work with a marriage.

"I understand. But what of your reputation?" Harriet squeezed her arm, her brow crinkled with worry.

Tibby shrugged. "I will survive, even if my reputation does not."

"What a disaster. I feel as if part of this is my fault. Each time I try to explain our *For Better or Worse* agenda, I make it sound terrible."

"Don't think that for a moment. Our plan is difficult to explain to others. I think Mother and Aunt Eleanor understand for the most part, but I wonder if Lady Trafford does. Then again, I haven't had a chance to speak with Michael about it, let alone his mother."

"If Captain Shaw is gone, perhaps now would be a good time to try."

Tibby shook her head, having already considered doing so. "To what end? While I don't want her to think poorly of me, Michael is the one who matters. Her loyalty is with him."

"True. What a terrible tangle. One I do not know how to unknot."

"Nor do I. Now that Michael has left, I'm not sure what will come of it."

"How long will he be gone?"

"The footman didn't know. Nor does he know where he went or why. I'm certain his mother does but of course I can't ask her."

"Hopefully, your maid will be able to find out eventually. What then?"

"I don't know." Tibby's shoulders sank as hopelessness threatened once again like an unwelcome fog, heavy and smothering. "How disheartening that I finally convinced Mother to consider attending a few events only to be uncertain whether we will be invited to any."

"That's ridiculous. People will soon forget all of this if they've even heard about it." Harriet scowled. "Perhaps we should have allowed Lady Lucinda and Lady Jane into the literary league after all."

"I don't think that would've made them act kinder toward us. Besides, we couldn't have any true conversations while they were present. They both admitted they don't like to read."

Harriet nodded. "You're right. But I can think of no other way to quiet them."

"I fear they will take every possible opportunity to tell others about this." Tibby paused to face Harriet. "I'm sorry that it will reflect poorly on all of our members, including you."

"Nonsense." Harriet waved a gloved hand in dismissal. "It will bring more attention to our little group, but maybe something positive will come from that just as it did for Phoebe." She smiled. "The news alone might be enough to make gentlemen look at us twice if they learn we're members. A bold move may not be necessary for the rest of us."

Tibby smiled. "Somehow, I don't think you'll escape your mission so easily." She watched as her friend's expression turned pensive, making Tibby wonder at her thoughts.

"Frances asked me to stop by after I visit with you."

Sensing there was more to the statement than was obvious, Tibby asked, "For a specific reason?"

"To discuss her idea." Harriet sighed. "I know you said I didn't have to wait until she finished before starting mine, but I can't seem to talk myself into acting."

"If you're like me, any reason to procrastinate is welcome."

"Perhaps that's it," Harriet said with a smile.

"I stand by what I said despite what happened. Move forward before it's too late. Though I don't recommend a pretend betrothal."

Harriet offered a sympathetic look. "I shall be certain to avoid that. None of us are getting any younger, are we? I can't believe we've all had five Seasons already. Where does the time go?"

Tibby looked back at her house, hating to think how long she'd spent inside those walls or how many more years were ahead of her. That wouldn't matter if she were happy or even content. But with Michael gone, the chance of that had been snuffed out like a candle flame in the wind.

"I do have some good news," Harriet added. "My uncle has asked if we could call on you and your mother. Do you think that would be acceptable?"

"I'm sure it would. Perhaps the day after tomorrow? That will give me time to prepare Mother."

"Perfect. He thought her charming. Isn't that sweet?"

"Especially considering her upset so soon after they met."

"We were all upset," Harriet added. "He blamed the sisters, as do I."

Tibby agreed though she knew she was at fault as well.

"One other good thing has come out of this experience," Tibby said. "I've realized that the last few years, I've believed I'm not enough." She paused to face Harriet again. "But I am. And so are you. We are enough just as we are. If the man for whom we care can't see that, then it's his loss." She gave a single nod to emphasize her point. If only her heart believed it.

"You are right. Brilliant, in fact." Harriet touched her hand again. "Thank you for sharing that. I hope you have the chance to speak with your captain. Regardless of the outcome, you should tell him what's in your heart."

"Perhaps I'll write him a letter and better explain everything. That seems to be the only way I'll have the chance." But Tibby didn't intend to tell him how she felt. Not when it would only make him feel sorry for her.

Her chest ached at the thought. She loved Michael with all her heart. But it would be better to live without him than have him marry her out of pity.

Chapter Twenty

"Thank you again, Shaw," Major Winters said as he shook Michael's hand. "May I call on you when the next opportunity arises?"

They'd just returned to London, having risen early to finish their journey. Though it was midday, no evidence of the sun broke through the low clouds that covered the city. Park Street was busy at this time of day, and Michael was anxious to return home.

"I'm sorry, but I believe my future lies elsewhere," Michael said. "I have a few other projects I will be spending time on instead."

"I'm sorry to hear that. Do let me know if your plans change."

"Of course."

"Good luck with your lady. I hope it works out."

"As do I." With a nod, Michael turned his horse toward home.

The trip had been a day longer than the last and consisted of taking a strongbox of valuables to York. While it had been even more lucrative than the previous one, it had also been more dangerous.

Though he couldn't deny the rush of adrenaline and determination that filled him when they'd been forced to fight off thieves, Michael didn't relish the thought of experiencing it again. Providing security for the transport of items didn't give him the sense of purpose he wanted even if the payment was generous.

However, the money he'd earned between both jobs would provide a solid start for the future.

A future with Tibby.

Time on the road had once again given him ample opportunity to think, and he'd come to several realizations.

He should've asked Tibby what she'd meant when she'd spoken of affection. Instead, he'd suggested they marry and for the wrong reason.

He heaved a sigh at his stupidity. His only excuse was that he'd been too worried that Tibby would tell him she'd suggested their betrothal only because of the literary league. That he'd been a convenient and safe option since they were already friends. After all, friends had affection for one another. He hoped that wasn't all she felt for him.

He also should've told her how much he cared for her that evening in the greenhouse when they'd shared those moments of passion. Instead, he'd allowed desire to control his actions rather than sharing his feelings.

While he'd been willing to admit how badly he'd botched everything, it had taken a conversation with Major Winters to better understand what was behind his actions.

"Our value doesn't depend on our deeds, but on who we are," Winters had said. "From what you've told me, your lady went to great lengths to catch your notice. That's the only explanation since it sounds as if she didn't actually need your help."

"Or did she choose me merely because I was convenient and allowed her to satisfy the literary league's challenge?"

"You'll have to determine that. But if you think you have a chance at love, seize it with both hands and hold tight. It's a gift not to be taken lightly and will enrich your life in ways you've never imagined."

Michael pondered the major's advice for a long while and realized he was guilty of gauging his self-worth based on what he accomplished. That was part of the reason he'd helped Tibby—to make himself feel better and ease the restlessness that had settled over him upon his return home.

While he didn't know how the situation with Tibby would resolve itself, he knew what he wanted. He hoped to share that with her. He also owed her an apology. He hoped they could move past all that had happened. He wanted to be more than merely convenient. He wanted her to love him.

His future wouldn't be complete if she wasn't in it. Did that mean he loved her? Absolutely. With all that he was.

"A letter arrived during your absence, Captain," the butler advised upon his return home.

One glance at the handwriting told him it was from Tibby. A rush of longing had him drawing a deep breath. His reaction made him even more certain of what he wanted.

He tucked the letter in his pocket without reading it, and greeted his mother and grandmother before cleaning up, eager to remove the dust from the road.

Only then did he pull out the letter, reluctant to open it. He'd much rather talk to Tibby in person than read what she'd written.

If she was willing to see him after his regrettable behavior.

In truth, it didn't matter what she'd said because he loved her and wanted her as his wife. He also wanted to apologize. He should've stood by her side at the garden party rather than leave. And he should've shared his feelings long before then. None of this would've happened if he had. Or at least, it wouldn't have caused a rift between them.

He returned to where his mother was in her sitting room, reading. "I'm going to call on Tibby."

"I'm pleased to hear that. Did your trip provide you with enough time to know what you intend to do?"

"Yes, it did." He smiled. "We shall see if it aligns with what Tibby wants."

"I will hope for good news." Her eyes were warm as was her smile. "Good luck."

He bent to kiss her cheek. "Thank you for your understanding through all this."

"You are an intelligent man. I had no doubt you'd come to the proper conclusion."

He turned to go.

"Michael, remember, you don't need to rescue Tabitha. She is a strong, capable woman with a purpose of her own."

He had to marvel at the clever women who surrounded him. "You are right, Mother."

Letter in hand, he strode out the door, anxious to see Tibby, noting the way his heart stirred at the thought of her.

He only hoped she was home, for he didn't think he could wait another moment to be with her.

"Good afternoon, Captain Shaw," the butler greeted him with a smile and a bow. "Lady Tabitha, Lady Dunford, and

Mrs. Cameron are entertaining guests in the drawing room at the moment."

The news was a pleasant surprise. Tibby must be thrilled that her mother was receiving guests. But he couldn't wait for a better time. Not when his palms were damp, and his heart threatened to beat out of his chest. "Perfect. No need to announce me."

Before the butler could reply, Michael strode toward the stairs.

TIBBY WATCHED IN AMAZEMENT as her mother giggled like a girl at something Mr. Hancock said. Tibby glanced at Harriet to see the same astonishment on her face.

"What is happening?" Harriet whispered.

"I'm not sure. I've never seen my mother act like this." Tibby noted Aunt Eleanor had the same look of surprise.

Mr. Hancock seemed as intrigued by her mother as she was by him based on his intent regard.

The butler had already brought in the tea tray and Tibby had poured once it became apparent that her mother hadn't noticed the tea's arrival.

"Have you always lived in London, Mr. Hancock?" Tibby asked. That was only the beginning of what she wanted to know but hoped he'd take her question as an invitation to tell them more about himself.

"I moved here from Lincolnshire after my wife passed away nine years ago." He shared a smile with Lady Chapman. "My sister suggested it, so I would be closer to family."

He continued to share other details of his life, and Tibby liked him even more as he spoke. He'd obviously been fond of his wife but seemed ready to move forward since he only spoke of happy times.

He soon turned the conversation to her mother, causing Tibby to hold her breath. Would she talk about her most recent illness or how much she missed her husband?

"My husband died seven years ago," her mother began. "We miss him dearly, of course."

She glanced at Tibby, who waited to see what else she might say.

"However, he'd want us to move on with our lives and find happiness." Her mother's lip trembled for a moment before she smiled.

Tibby couldn't have been prouder.

"Do you enjoy music, Mr. Hancock?" her mother asked with a surprising change of subject.

Lady Chapman joined the conversation, and Tibby, at last, allowed herself to relax and her thoughts to wander. As always, they turned to Michael. From what she knew, he was still gone. Would he return soon, or might it be months before he came home?

The thought was a dismal one.

She'd written him a letter to more fully explain why she'd suggested the pretend betrothal, though she would've preferred to tell him in person. But with each day that passed, her hope for a reconciliation dimmed a little more. How she wished she'd been brave enough to share what was in her heart before the garden party. Then perhaps he'd have reacted differently despite what Lady Lucinda and Lady Jane had said.

"Isn't that right, Tabitha?"

She looked at her mother, realizing she'd lost track of the conversation.

Before she could respond, Harriet released a quiet gasp. Tibby followed her friend's gaze to the doorway where Michael stood.

Surprise gripped her as she drank in his presence, noting he held a letter in his hand—her letter if she wasn't mistaken. Her heart leapt to her throat and lodged there.

"Michael." She jerked to her feet as the room fell silent.

His gaze shifted to take in the others in the room. "My apologies for interrupting."

He'd never looked better, perhaps because she'd missed him so. His dark hair held a slight wave, brushing the collar of his brown suit coat. His skin looked bronzed as if he'd been in the sun more than usual. But it was the intensity in his green eyes that caught her.

She wished she knew what he was thinking, but his expression was unreadable. Though he'd hurt her, she was also to blame for the misunderstanding. She should've been honest with him from the start.

Tibby waited a long, painful moment but still, he didn't speak. She stepped forward, gripping her hands tightly lest she be tempted to reach for him. "Did you wish to speak with me?"

Please say yes. Please say yes. Please say yes, she repeated silently.

She glanced behind her to see everyone riveted to the scene unfolding before them, and then looked back to Michael. "We could step into another room," she suggested since he had yet to say anything.

"I received your letter but haven't opened it," he said as if he hadn't heard her.

Tibby's heart sank, disappointment that he hadn't bothered to read her explanation threatening to overwhelm her. She swallowed against the well of emotion in her throat, telling herself that was all right. She could tell him now—if he'd listen.

"There's something you should know first," he said, stuffing the letter in his pocket as he walked closer until he stood before her.

She fisted a hand in the fabric of her gown in an effort to brace herself for whatever he was about to say.

"I love you," he blurted. "I know we have issues to discuss. I owe you an apology and so much more. But I want you to know that I love you. I would like to spend the rest of my life showing you how much." He took her hand and dropped to one knee. "Will you do me the honor of marrying me?"

Harriet's gasp was even louder than Tibby's.

"Aren't they already betrothed?" Lady Chapman whispered.

Everything else in the room faded as Tibby looked into Michael's eyes, her heart filling with love. She squeezed his hand, wishing they were alone so she could say everything in her heart. For now, a simple response would have to do. "I love you, too. Yes, I would like that more than anything."

His immediate grin had her responding in kind. He stood, and everyone joined them to offer congratulations, starting with Tibby's mother.

"I am pleased for you." Her mother hugged Tibby and leaned back to meet her gaze. "I do want you to be happy, dear. I'm sorry to have made you think otherwise." She glanced between them. "I want you both to be happy. This time it's real, isn't it?"

"Yes," Michael answered, sharing a smile with Tibby.

"Welcome to the family, Michael," her mother added.

"Perhaps a pretend betrothal wasn't such a bad idea after all," Harriet whispered when she hugged Tibby. "Just wait until Phoebe and the other league members hear the good news."

Once everyone returned to their seats, Michael looked at Tibby. "Shall we share the good news with my mother?"

"I would like that." She turned to the others. "If you'll excuse us for a few minutes."

"Of course," Tibby's mother said, though her lips tightened before she turned her attention back to Mr. Hancock.

Tibby knew she and her mother had a long road ahead of them still, but she appreciated that her mother was trying.

Michael tucked Tibby's hand under his arm, and they started down the stairs together. "Shall we walk through the garden on our way?"

Tibby nodded, thrilled to think they could steal a few minutes alone.

The moment they were out the door and past a tall hedge that allowed them some privacy, Michael halted to take both her hands in his. "Can you forgive me?"

"Only if you can forgive me. I would like to tell you everything that I didn't before."

"Of course. I'm sorry I didn't allow you the opportunity to earlier." He shook his head. "I feared you had suggested the betrothal because I provided a convenient way for you to fulfill your literary league's plan. When you mentioned your affection for me, I assumed you meant friendship." He released her hand to trail a finger along her cheek. "I hope that I wasn't simply an easy solution."

"Not at all. The *For Better or Worse* agenda is to help encourage each of us to do something to catch the eye of the man for whom we've carried a secret *tendre*. To help them see us differently." She dropped her gaze, aware of the heat filling her cheeks. "You see, I have been in love with you for a long time."

"Tibby."

She looked up, hoping not to see pity in his expression. To her relief, all she saw was love.

"I am blessed beyond belief. Thank goodness you suggested the betrothal, or I might not have realized what was in front of me all along. You. The love of my life. The lady with whom I want to spend every moment of every day. Who makes me a better man than I was before. Who believes I can do anything, including writing a book."

Tibby laughed. "Because you can."

"We shall see. I intend to try. But only with you at my side. I love you so very much."

"Oh, Michael. You are the only man I will ever love. You've helped me realize that I deserve happiness and that I am worthy of love. Without you, I wouldn't have been brave enough to reach for more."

"We are going to have a wonderful life together." He drew her close and took her mouth with his, the kiss so gentle and sweet that it weakened her knees even as it made her heart soar.

MICHAEL ARRIVED AT the Rowden Ball a week later with one goal in mind—to silence anyone who questioned whether his betrothal to Tibby was real. He hoped to accomplish it without saying a word. What better way to end any gossip than by showing those who cared to notice just how much he adored his soon-to-be bride?

"What has you looking so fierce this evening?" his mother asked quietly as they entered the ballroom.

"I am in search of those sisters who caused such trouble at the garden party."

His mother drew to a halt in alarm. "You don't intend to confront them, do you?"

"Of course not. Nothing so uncivilized." Michael smiled. "I only want to make certain they see how madly in love I am with Tibby."

The look of approval his mother sent him only made him smile more. "You haven't looked this happy since you returned home."

He would admit to feeling a certain smugness. "I am very happy, not to mention lucky." His gaze found Tibby, who was just arriving with her mother. "Thanks to Tibby."

She was his reason for striving to be more. Not because she required his help. In truth, he was certain that he needed her more than she needed him.

She looked over the crowd and found him at once as if they had a deep connection that bonded them in an elemental way.

He was eager to begin their life together. He'd already told her the reason behind his trips if not the full details. She'd been astonished that he had taken steps toward their future when it had been far from settled.

"Shall we join them?" he asked his mother.

"Yes. I want to hear how Pekoe is doing."

Michael chuckled. The little dog that Mr. Hancock had presented to Lady Dunford several days ago was adorable. The older gentleman had told Tibby he thought it might help Lady Dunford adjust to Tibby's upcoming marriage.

"I think we're going to have to find a dog for you, Mother."

"Only if it's as sweet and well-behaved as Pekoe."

"Good evening, Lady Dunford. Lady Tabitha." Michael bowed.

After the required pleasantries had been exchanged and his mother requested an update on Pekoe, Michael shifted closer to Tibby.

Her lavender gown had a rather daring neckline compared to what she normally wore. A band of ecru lace bordered the ruffles around the neckline, sleeves, and hem. Her hair was bound in a loose chignon that begged him to remove the unseen pins that held it.

He sighed, wondering if she had any idea of what she did to him. Their wedding couldn't come soon enough.

"You look more beautiful every time I see you," he whispered.

"Thank you." A hint of a color tinged her cheeks as she smiled, positively glowing with happiness.

Michael liked to think he had something to do with that. Then again, she was the reason he felt the same way.

"I'm going to have to find Mother a dog just like Pekoe," he said as he watched their mothers visit.

Tibby laughed. "Mr. Hancock should be here this evening. We'll have to ask him where he got her. She is a treasure." She glanced at her mother. "I wish I had thought to try a dog years ago."

"Thank goodness you didn't, or you might not have pretended to need me."

"I will always *need* you," she said quietly, a tenderness in her eyes that threatened to weaken his knees.

He offered his arm. "Would you care to dance?"

"Yes, please."

After excusing themselves, they moved slowly through the crowd, content to be with each other.

"If you're available tomorrow," Michael began, "my brother sent word of a townhouse for us to look at."

Tibby's eyes widened with excitement. "How exciting. Is it nearby?" She wanted to be as close to her mother as possible, although her brother and sister-in-law had already advised they'd be moving into the family home soon after Tibby's wedding.

"Only a few streets away. From what Markus told me, it sounds perfect for us with room for a family and a bedroom for your mother whenever she wants to stay."

"I can't wait to see it." She drew to a halt, her lashes fluttering as she looked away.

"What is it?" he asked as concern filled him.

"I can hardly believe we will soon be married," she whispered. She met his gaze again. "Each morning when I wake, I have to remind myself this isn't a dream."

He longed to take her into his arms and reassure her that it was very real. But he already felt the weight of looks from the other guests nearby. He settled for lifting her hand and pressing his lips to the oval ruby engagement ring she wore under her glove, a gift from his grandmother. "I find myself doing the same thing."

"Tibby?" a feminine voice said.

They turned to see a lady approaching. While she was unfamiliar to Michael, he knew the man at her side.

"Phoebe! I didn't realize you'd returned." Tibby hugged the new arrival, leaving Michael to bow then shake the offered hand of the Earl of Bolton.

"Shaw. Good to see you in London again," Bolton said with a smile.

"It's good to be here."

"I understand congratulations are in order from what my wife has told me." The earl lifted a brow, a teasing grin on his face. "You work quickly."

"I might say the same for you," Michael replied. "It doesn't sound as if you believe in lengthy betrothals either."

Bolton chuckled as he cast an adoring look at the dark-haired lady who spoke animatedly with Tibby. "What's the purpose of waiting when you know exactly what you want?"

"Agreed." Michael nodded.

"Phoebe, this is Captain Michael Shaw," Tibby said as she reached for Michael's arm. "Michael, may I introduce Phoebe Stanhope, the Countess of Bolton."

"It's a pleasure to meet you." Michael bowed. "I understand I have you to thank for the *For Better or Worse* agenda."

Lady Bolton's eyes went wide as she glanced between Tibby and Michael. Then she laughed as if realizing he actually was grateful. "You're quite welcome. I'm pleased it's worked so well thus far." The lady's attention caught on something just past Michael's shoulder.

He turned to see the two sisters who'd caused such a problem watching them closely. They stood near enough to have heard everything that had been said.

Tibby tightened her hold on his arm, and the urge to prove anything to them fell away. Nothing mattered but the lady at his side who held his heart.

"My love, did you invite Lord and Lady Bolton to our wedding?" he asked as he returned his focus to Tibby, easily ignoring the continued stares of the sisters.

Tibby's warm brown eyes held on him before she looked at the countess again. "Yes, we hope you can attend."

"I wouldn't miss it for the world," Lady Bolton said.

To his surprise, Tibby looked back to the two ladies who continued to watch with puzzled expressions. "Perhaps you'll be lucky enough to find love one day." She smiled, sharing a look with Michael. "I suggest you start in the pages of a book. It's amazing what a love of reading can bring."

The countess stepped forward. "Isn't it though? A passion for books can bring forth other passions as well."

"Passion and a bold move," Tibby added, love so clearly written on her face as she held his gaze that it caused Michael to catch his breath. "Who knew a pretend betrothal could lead to true love?"

"I'm so pleased it did. Forever and always." Michael grinned, his heart brimming with happiness. He truly was blessed.

Epilogue

5 *Years Later*
Tibby smiled at the sight of Michael hard at work at his desk in the sitting room that adjoined their bedroom even though night had fallen. The lamplight revealed the look of concentration furrowing his brow that often came over him when he was writing.

A lock of dark hair fell over his forehead as he wrote quickly, suggesting the words were flowing in his mind faster than he could keep up with on paper.

She'd already prepared for bed and slowly drew closer, not wanting to interrupt his thoughts but impatient to speak with him. She couldn't keep her news to herself for much longer.

At last, he blew out a breath as he set down the pen and leaned back in his chair with a satisfied look.

"I would guess the story is going well," she said as she came forward to run her hands along his broad shoulders clad only in his shirt.

"Better than I had hoped," he said, placing his hand over the top of hers as he looked at her and smiled. "There is not one murder victim, but two."

She couldn't help but laugh at the happiness the news brought him. "I look forward to reading it."

"Can you believe this is my third book?" He shook his head in disbelief. "If not for you, I wouldn't have attempted to write the first one." He pushed back from the desk and turned his chair then pulled her down on his lap.

She wrapped her arms around his neck and kissed his cheek. "I think you would have been called to writing eventually."

"I'm not so sure. But I do know the books wouldn't be nearly as good without your help." He tucked a strand of hair behind her ear, the tender look in his green eyes melting her heart.

"I thoroughly enjoy discussing ideas. The ladies in the literary league are excited that your second book has finally been published. They're hoping you'll be willing to speak with us about it after they read it."

He gave a mock shudder. "I am not sure if I would care to do that again."

"But you did so well with the first book," she protested. "That discussion went wonderfully."

"If you say so." His smile suggested she might be able to talk him into it.

"Just think of how many of their friends they will tell about the book. The more people who speak of it the better."

"I am lucky to get the book written, let alone try to find ways to sell copies of it."

"Which is why I do my best to assist you. Your publisher has already agreed to a larger printing of the second book."

"I'm anxious to hear whether readers like it."

"I have no doubt they will. I spoke with Mother earlier."

"Oh?"

"She's having dinner with Mr. Hancock this evening. Your mother and she went for their daily morning walk with their dogs earlier."

"I continue to be amazed by how attached they are to the dogs," he said, amusement lacing his tone.

"She also said your mother mentioned how wonderful your roses are blooming."

"They are? How surprising that they've survived considering my questionable botany skills."

She ran a finger along his forehead and down his cheek, appreciating the shadow of whiskers already visible, giving him a rugged look. "Are you done for the evening?"

"Yes," he said with a glance at the papers on his desk. "Did William settle down for the night? I didn't mean to stir him up when I said good night."

"He fell asleep before I finished the second page of the book we've been reading."

"Excellent. He had a busy day."

"Indeed, he did." Butterflies danced in her middle with the news she had to share. "Soon he will be even busier."

Michael frowned. "How so?"

Her smile bloomed along with the love in her heart.

Michael stared at her for a long moment as awareness dawned. "Are you saying what I think you're saying?"

She nodded and placed a hand on her still flat stomach. "Yes, I do believe so. We will be parents again soon after the new year."

"Darling Tabitha." His eyes darkened, and he tightened his hold on her, his forehead tipping forward to touch hers. "I am the luckiest man."

"And I am the luckiest woman."

He lifted his head to search her face. "How are you feeling?"

"Excellent and so, so happy."

"Wonderful. William is going to be thrilled to have a little brother or sister." He kissed her with such sweetness that it had her blinking back tears.

"I love you, Michael," she whispered.

"Good, because I love you, Tibby. You are my heart. Not a day goes by that I am not grateful that you suggested our pretend betrothal."

"A pretend betrothal ending in a true marriage." She grinned. "I don't think I would've been brave enough to do it without the aid of the literary league."

"How long is the waiting list to join these days?" he asked.

"Rather lengthy from what Phoebe said." The idea still amused her even after all this time. "Do you remember we're to dine with her and Bolton tomorrow evening?"

"Yes. I look forward to it. There's something else I'm looking forward to." He pressed kisses along her jaw and down her neck.

"Oh?" She shivered as desire stirred. "What might that be?" She leaned her head back, closing her eyes to better enjoy his attentions.

"Making love with you, Mrs. Shaw."

"I was hoping you would say that, my dear captain." She kissed him deeply, loving the way he made her feel.

His tongue thrust against hers as he ran a finger along the neckline of her nightgown.

Then he broke the kiss and stood, cradling her in his arms.

"Michael," she said with a gasp as she tightened her arms around his neck.

"Yes, my love?" He carried her into their bedroom where the covers were already turned down on the bed and laid her on it.

"Did I mention how much I love you?" she whispered.

"Yes, but tell me again." He held her gaze, the heat in them stirring her further.

"I love you with every beat of my heart and every breath I take. Forever and a day." It was impossible to imagine her life without Michael.

"Tibby." He closed his eyes briefly as if overcome by emotion. Then he opened them again, and the love in his expression caused her heart to swell. "Each time I think I couldn't possibly love you more, I am proven wrong. You are my heart and soul. Always."

He kissed her again, his hand moving to her stomach where the life they'd created together grew inside her, holding there for a moment. She placed her hand on top of his.

"You are a wonderful mother," he said, the tender look in his eyes warming her from head to toe.

"We are wonderful parents," Tibby countered as she unbuttoned his shirt, anxious to feel him against her.

As if he shared the same need, he straightened to toe off his shoes, tug the shirt over his head, and unfasten his trousers, tossing them aside.

Then he joined her on the bed. The warmth of his hand caressing her through the thin nightgown had never felt so good.

She trailed her fingers along his muscled shoulder and arm, over his hair-covered chest then down to the flat plane of his stomach.

He drew a quick breath when she grasped his stiff manhood. "Tibby."

"Yes?"

"You are a siren," he muttered then drew her nightgown over her head. His gaze roamed over her body in the dim light. "Perfect." His hands followed his gaze, along with his mouth, lifting her passion ever higher. He cradled her breast and took the erect nipple into his mouth while his hand danced along her belly then lower still.

She opened for him, welcoming his intimate touch. "You make me feel wonderful."

"The pleasure is mine," he said while he continued the sweet torture.

Her hips bucked when need took hold. "Now, Michael." She reached for him to pull him on top of her, loving the weight of his body on hers.

"Yes," he practically growled. He settled between her legs, the tip of his staff touching her center before pushing forward.

As one, they paused, looking into each other's eyes in a moment of unity.

"My love," Michael whispered. Then he kissed her and moved against hers in a steady rhythm, bringing them both closer and closer to completion. His hand touched her shoulder, her breast, her waist, leaving a path of heat in its wake. Then he shifted onto his elbow to caress her slick folds.

Her body grew taut as she hovered on the edge before at last spilling over, taking him with her as they shattered together.

They slowly descended back to earth, both breathing heavily. Michael rolled to the side and drew her into his arms. "I love you, my darling wife."

She sighed, amazed at the happiness that hummed inside her. "And I love you, Michael. Always and forever."

The End

ORDER A MISTAKEN IDENTITY, Book 3 of The Mayfair Literary League, today, coming May 2023.

How far would you go in the name of friendship?

A terrible secret...

Lady Harriet Persimmons stopped dreaming of love long ago. Her stepfather's cruelty left her with scars that are only part of what makes her unlovable. Yet one man has caught her admiration even if he's out of reach.

To Harriet's dismay, her shy friend Frances carries a torch for the same gentleman. Even worse, Frances asks for Harriet's help to gain his notice at a house party.

Joseph Harris, Viscount Garland, attends the party with one goal—to convince his wealthy host to invest in his new venture. The sweet yet seductive messages he receives from the man's daughter catch him off guard even as they intrigue him. But the notes don't seem match the lady herself, and her lovely friend is the one who captures his interest.

A mistaken identity...

Each moment Harriet spends with Joseph trying to convince him why Frances is perfect for him has her heart more and more entangled. The kiss they share is a terrible mistake, but one she can't forget.

Will a mistaken identity end with the chance for a happily ever after?

Order your copy of A MISTAKEN IDENTITY and follow the ladies of the Mayfair Literary League as they pursue their happily ever afters!

Other Books by Lana Williams

The Mayfair Literary League:
A Matter of Convenience, Book 1
A Pretend Betrothal, Book 2
A Mistaken Identity, Book 3
The Duke's Lost Treasures:
Once Upon a Duke's Wish, Book 1
A Kiss from the Marquess, Book 2
If Not for the Duke, Book 3
The Seven Curses of London Series:
Trusting the Wolfe, a Novella, Book .5
Loving the Hawke, Book I
Charming the Scholar, Book II
Rescuing the Earl, Book III
Dancing Under the Mistletoe, a Christmas Novella, Book IV
Tempting the Scoundrel, a Novella, Book V
Falling For the Viscount, Book VI
Daring the Duke, Book VII
Wishing Upon A Christmas Star, a Novella, Book VIII
Ruby's Gamble, a Novella
Gambling for the Governess, Book IX
Redeeming the Lady, Book X
Enchanting the Duke, Book XI

The Seven Curses of London Boxset (Books 1-3)
The Secret Trilogy:
Unraveling Secrets, Book I
Passionate Secrets, Book II
Shattered Secrets, Book III
The Secret Trilogy Boxset (Books 1-3)
The Rogue Chronicles
Romancing the Rogue, Book 1
A Rogue's Reputation, a Christmas Novella, Book 2
A Rogue No More, Book 3
A Rogue to the Rescue, Book 4
A Rogue and Some Mistletoe, a Christmas Novella, Book
5
To Dare A Rogue, Book 6
A Rogue Meets His Match, Book 7
The Rogue's Autumn Bride, Book 8
A Rogue's Christmas Kiss, a Christmas Novella, Book 9
A Rogue's Redemption, a short story, Book 10
A Match Made in the Highlands, a Novella
Medieval Romances:
Falling for A Knight Series:
A Knight's Christmas Wish, Novella, Book .5
A Knight's Quest, Book 1 (Also available in Audio)
A Knight's Temptation, Book 2 (Also available in Audio)
A Knight's Captive, Book 3 (Also available in Audio)
The Vengeance Trilogy:
A Vow To Keep, Book I
A Knight's Kiss, Novella, Book 1.5
Trust In Me, Book II
Believe In Me, Book III

Contemporary Romances:
Yours for the Weekend, a Novella

IF YOU ENJOYED THIS story, I invite you to sign up to my newsletter on my website at lanawilliams.net to find out when the next one is released. I'd be honored if you'd consider writing a review! Join my private VIP Readers Group on Facebook for fun conversations, sneak peeks, giveaways, and more!

About the Author

L ana Williams is a USA Today Bestselling Author who writes historical romance filled with mystery, adventure, and sometimes a pinch of paranormal to stir things up. She spends her days in days in Victorian, Regency, and Medieval times, depending on her mood and current deadline.

Lana writes in the Rocky Mountains with her husband, two spoiled dogs, and loves hearing from readers. Stop by her website at lanawilliams.net and say hello! You can also connect with her on Facebook, Twitter, or Instagram. Join her private VIP Readers Group on Facebook for fun conversations, sneak peeks, and giveaways!

Made in the USA
Monee, IL
28 August 2023

41747007R00156